Watercolours

Ron Ranson's
PAINTING
SCHOOL

Watercolours

RON RANSON

BROCKHAMPTON PRESS
LONDON

First published in Great Britain in 1993 by
Anaya Publishers Ltd., Strode House,
44–50 Osnaburgh Street, London, NW1 3ND.

This edition published 1995 by Brockhampton Press,
a member of Hodder Headline PLC Group

Managing Editor: Delian Bower
Text Editor: Helen Douglas-Cooper
Art Director: Jane Forster
Design Assistant: Sarah Willis
Photography: Shona Wood

British Library Cataloguing in Publication Data
Ranson, Ron
Watercolours - (Ron Ranson's Painting
School Series)
I. Title II. Series
751.42

ISBN 1 86019 176 2

Typeset in Great Britain by
Bookworm Typesetting, Manchester
Colour reproduction by J. Film Process, Singapore
Printed and bound by Oriental Press, Dubai

Front cover: View of harbour, Port Clyde, Maine, USA.
Title page: View of harbour at low tide.

Contents

THE ELEMENTS

Introduction

Like me, some of you may have come late to painting, thinking perhaps that it's almost too late and wishing you had started sooner. Perhaps as a child you were keen and showed some talent, but by the time you left school, for all sort of reasons, you had lost interest. Perhaps it was poor teaching, or maybe your inhibitions took over. Young children start off completely fearless, full of exciting ideas, and happy to put lots of colour on paper joyously and with abandon.

Unfortunately, however, at about the age of eight, all this is taken away from them and they're given sharp pencils, rubbers and coloured crayons, or perhaps little scholastic boxes of paint, hard pens and tiny cheap, almost invisible brushes to work with. No wonder people lose interest and become bored with the whole process of ART. My aim is to recreate this earlier joyous abandon, and get you to throw away your inhibitions – in other words, get back to the inexpensive paints and big brushes. I feel I can help you do this, as what I've described was exactly what happened to me.

Art was my only good subject at school, but I was discouraged by the teachers and was told that I'd never make a living at it and should go and do something sensible like engineering. I then wasted upwards of 30 years before losing my job at 50. This freed me to start a whole new career in art, or to be more specific, watercolour. Never having had any training, I was able to leap in without any inhibitions, developing my own set of unconventional materials and techniques, which helped me to paint in a loose and free way right from the start, recapturing that childhood abandon.

My whole life was changed, and now with no office to go to, I'm free to roam the world, teaching and passing on my ideas to enthusiastic students everywhere through my workshop, books and videos. I've never been happier! The fact of having a late start and no training has helped rather than hindered, because it has enabled me to relate to and establish a link with my students. I can't emphasize enough, that the kind of painting I want to teach you is *attainable* by practically everyone. You don't need special talent or that dreadful word "gift" which is often bandied about!

Painting is to a large extent like any other craft or even sport, like knitting, typing, crocheting, tennis or carpentry. We all appear hamfisted and inept when we start any of them. We may even make a fool of ourselves at the beginning. I certainly did when I started downhill skiing at 65. But if you are humble enough to accept this temporary loss of dignity, and are willing to persevere, nothing on earth will stop you becoming a competent artist – maybe not a great one. Just because some of us will never win at Wimbledon, it needn't stop us from dreaming of gaining a cup in the mixed doubles in our local tennis club. However, we must keep practising our backhand strokes and our serves, or we'll stay a "rabbit" for ever. I can tell very quickly those of my students who are going to make it – not the seemingly talented ones who paint when they feel like it, but the ones who patiently, for hours, learn to practise with the rigger. They're the ones who in a year or so will be running their own classes, or having one-man shows.

If you happen to like some of the work in this book, and wish to paint similar kinds of pictures, I promise that you can! – I just need some concentration and perseverance from you in return, and we'll both make it!

This painting of a fast-moving stream may look complicated, but I painted it with just three brushes and a limited number of colours. I put in the background wet into wet with dilute colour, and gradually strengthened the colour as I worked forwards. I used the brushes to create a variety of marks that convey the trees, the suggested forms of the rocks in the stream, and the water itself. I left areas of the paper bare to suggest patches of light on the water.

THE BASICS

I've read so many books on watercolour and have a very large library, all well thumbed, having been read by the hundreds of students who I have taught over the years. Many of these books recommend buying the very best possible, and therefore the most expensive, art materials from the start. For example, genuine sable brushes in various sizes, hand-made watercolour paper and, of course, professional artists' quality paints. The result is, that faced with these expensive products, you're intimidated to say the least. You're afraid to squeeze the paint out generously, afraid to spoil that lovely virgin paper, and things lie around for months waiting for you to screw up enough courage to make a start. Having been through all this myself at the beginning, I really can sympathize.

My own set of materials is designed to try to do away with much of this fear. I've ruthlessly cut the number of them down to the bone, hopefully making it easier for you to concentrate your skill on handling these few remaining tools and colours.

I truly believe that these materials are perfectly adequate for any aspiring artist, and in fact I use them all myself. The colours I use are made by a world famous manufacturer and are just as permanent as the more expensive artists' colours.

Many students have been led to believe that cheaper paints will fade more quickly, but this is not true. The large tubes I use have the effect of making you less mean with the paint, and with so few colours, it's possible to become conversant with the mixes far more quickly.

As to the brushes, I gave up using expensive sables years ago, having found that the cost of the brush had little effect on my painting!

I use machine-made paper rather than hand-made. It is acid free, and I also found the sizing on the hand-made paper a bit off-putting, as well as the price being intimidating when you come to use it.

This scene painted quickly on the spot in Venice demonstrates well the use of the hake and rigger. After putting in the sky with the hake, the buildings, awnings and tables were done with the 1in flat. The figures were finally added with the rigger, and the shadows with the hake.

Materials

Let's look at the paints first. So many amateur painters buy lots of exotically named colours including made-up mauves, pinks and greens in the mistaken hope that it will save mixing them. They probably keep them in a big bag, and after tipping them out will peer at the tiny labels trying to find just the right hue. They've spent a fortune on them and they're still in trouble!

My method is to use only seven and get nice fat tubes so that you're not afraid to squeeze them out.

Just put two of them together, and you'll still get subtle mauves, pinks and greens and in far less time. What's more, rather than having a lot of vague acquaintances, you'll have a few close friends, and you'll quickly get to know how they'll react with one another. The seven colours are raw sienna, lemon yellow, paynes grey, ultramarine, burnt umber, alizarin crimson and light red, and I recommend that you buy them in 21ml tubes (see List of Suppliers, page 128).

Shown below are the main materials. First the white plastic tray and the seven 21ml tubes of colours. The three main brushes are the hake, the No 3 rigger and the 1in flat, and the two top ones are the No 24 round brush which I use for flower paintings, and the small hog's hair brush used for softening and corrections. Finally, there's the collapsible water pot.

THE BRUSHES

For most of my painting I use only three brushes, the hake, the 1in flat (a few makes are described as 25mm) and the No 3 rigger, which are described on the next few pages. You'll also see two more in the illustration below. One is a No 24 round brush (see page 120) which I use only for my flower painting, and the other is a small hog's hair brush normally used for oil painting, but which I use with clean water for softening edges or removing paint. Although the hog's hair is abrasive enough to take the paint off, it won't damage the paper if done gently.

As for my palette, I prefer to use a large white plastic or metal butcher's tray from an ironmongers, as I find that the proprietary palettes in art shops usually have little compartments which get filled with dry paint. I like to squeeze fresh paint out each time I paint.

Next comes paper. I find that the more expensive and hand-made it is, the more intimidating it seems to be. I always use a machine-made paper because it is less expensive than hand-made ones. I choose a heavy paper of about 300gsm (140lb), which is thick

enough not to cockle when it's wet. This type of paper is available in different sizes in handy wire-bound books of twelve sheets with a cardboard backing. As for stretching paper, this has become something of a ritual which occupies a lot of time. I've never done it myself as I feel that it makes the paper even more intimidating to use. Paper of course does expand when wet, but if it's allowed to expand and contract without hindrance, as it can when you are working in a watercolour pad, it will dry flat.

Those are all the actual painting materials needed and the rest of my equipment is equally simple and straightforward. I have a tubular metal easel for painting outside, with a collapsible plastic waterpot that hangs on it. I then carry everything around in a plastic fisherman's box. All this should be easily obtainable in any art shop. Finally, you need a rag.

If you have trouble finding any of the materials mentioned, try the firms listed on page 126.

DO'S AND DONT'S

Do use your paint generously.

Do use both sides of the paper – if you fail on one side, you may succeed on the back, as I often do, probably because you feel less inhibited.

Do put the tops back on your tubes of paint. It's no good grumbling at the manufacturer if the paint goes hard.

Do, if using pads of paper as I do, paint straight on the pad, then you won't need to use drawing pins or sticky tape.

Do use fresh paint every time. Dry hard paint is useless, and it wears your brushes out.

Don't leave your palette with old paint on it. Try to keep it fresh and sparkling.

Don't leave the paint to go hard in the brushes or you'll be faced with rock hard bristles.

Don't forget you'll need plenty of clean rags.

Don't use too much water or the paint can get out of control.

THE HAKE

The key to my approach to watercolour is the hake, a large flat brush traditionally made in the Far East from goat hair. You either love it or hate it! At first glance it looks big, crude and unwieldy – you will probably think it impossible to paint delicate sensitive watercolours with, so why not use a nice little springy sable with a sharp point? The trouble with the sable is that it presents a tremendous temptation to "fiddle" – that most common disease of the watercolour painter. The hake, by its very nature and size, doesn't allow this and literally forces you to simplify your washes and eliminate fussy detail.

The main problem is the amount of water the hake holds. If you immerse it entirely in the waterpot, it then floods the palette preventing you from getting good rich washes. A large paint rag in the other hand is the answer! I'm continually dabbing my hake on it to remove the excess water before I mix my paint. Furthermore, when I've started painting I just put the tip of the brush in the water so it does not pick up too much.

Once you've conquered the water problem the brush becomes more manageable. Also, I'm continually "honing" mine on the palette, partly to keep the hairs together and in the long term to sharpen the brush. It certainly improves with age, getting sharper and more controllable, like a chef's knife. Of course there are good and bad hakes made in Japan, China and Taiwan, at various prices. (The Taiwan ones seem to be more crude and cheaper.)

Hold the brush lightly and delicately and touch the paper as lightly as a feather – the less you disturb the paper the fresher the watercolour. The hake won't ever be able to do crisp sharp marks or delicate branches. It's not intended for that, but it's marvellous for loose skies, trees and dramatic foregrounds. I suppose I do about 80 per cent of my own paintings with it.

You're not going to learn to use it or even feel comfortable with it in an hour or so. You'll need to persevere and practise. If you're fainthearted or impatient it will probably finish up in a drawer unloved and unseen, but if you stick to it and continue to practise from the exercises in this book, you'll never want to be without it.

The corner is used, flicking it up in an arc to give an impression of undergrowth.

As you can see, nearby trees can be indicated by using tiny sideways movements with the edge of the brush while moving it upwards.

This is a firm stroke used a lot for beaches and the foreshores of lakes. It's a very fast, light stroke that gives ready-made texture. Practise this a lot – it's very useful.

This picture is done entirely with the hake to show its versatility. First of all, put on a pale bluey-green wash over the whole of the background and then add strong, rich greens at each side using thicker paint, made from paynes grey and lemon yellow. The white trees can be scratched out with a fingernail or the end of a brush while the paint is still damp.

When the top half of your painting is dry, you can add the foreground foliage with the heel of the brush. The ground at the bottom can be done with warmer greens (made by adding raw sienna), and you'll get the shadows by mixing ultramarine and light red.

This stroke creates beautiful distant mountains. Start from the left using the edge of the brush and when you reach the peak, twist it slightly.

Gentle taps with the back and side of the brush, almost like stippling, will enable you to indicate convincing foliage. Don't do this with too wet a brush.

Here I'm using the corner of the hake very gently with downward strokes to indicate foliage. I'm working wet into wet at the bottom.

THE 1in FLAT BRUSH

This brush has an entirely different character from the hake. It's made of man-made fibre, and is very sharp and springy, as opposed to the hake's more malleable goat hair. It's ideal for doing tonal sketches in burnt umber before you start your final paintings. I love to sketch with it, and again, once you've practised with it you'll enjoy using it. Just look at the vignettes on these pages done entirely with this brush, and you'll realize its versatility. I hold it and use it very lightly, hardly touching the paper, whilst continually changing the angle from vertical to horizontal, with a little sideways stroke here and there.

If I want a fine line like a ship's mast or a gate, I just touch the edge of the brush lightly on the paper, joining it with another stroke to make it longer, or tilting the brush over, to make a shorter line. Small windows can be indicated by just touching the paper with the corner, which gives a wedge-shaped mark, while for roofs I make staccato marks, using the flat of the brush at an angle. For roofs in the distance, just one touch of the flat is enough. You can make whole towns up in seconds, see page 104.

Just look at the buildings in the paintings on page 10, and you'll see how comparatively complex architectural subjects that would take hours to do with a normal pointed brush, can be indicated

freshly and simply with the 1in flat. Railings on balconies, docks, boats, tiny chimneys, all can be achieved with a feather-light touch, and it's obviously easier to handle than the hake. However, don't expect it to do everything any more than you'd expect to hammer a nail in with a screwdriver. It does its own job superbly, portraying man-made objects, and its sharp marks contrast well with the soft, rough marks of the hake. Combined with the rigger, it covers most situations and subjects.

By just touching the edge of the flat gently on the paper, you'll get the effect of railings etc. By joining the lines you can achieve masts for yachts.

Little rowing boats are produced by putting in a top line with the edge of the brush, leaving a gap, and then putting in downward strokes.

You can get nice flourishes by simply swinging the brush in an arc while twisting it slightly – useful for small beaches and so on.

These illustrations are done with the flat brush. In the one above the mountains are a weak mixture of light red and ultramarine modified on the right with raw sienna. The windows are created by just touching in with the corner of the brush. The beach is put in lightly to get the textured effect. The shadow on the building is again light red and ultramarine.

A nice dry-brush effect is obtained by moving the brush very quickly across the paper. I find this stroke useful for walls.

If you use the corner of the brush you'll get convincing doors, windows etc. without too much detail. You don't need to indicate every window in a street.

The scene at the top was done almost entirely with light red, ultramarine and raw sienna. First put on a thin wash for the distant hills, followed by stronger washes for the foreground buildings. I couldn't resist adding the figure with the rigger. The foreground path can be put in very quickly and lightly to get the texture.

The little scene above is a mixture of paynes grey, raw sienna, light red and ultramarine. To get the reflections in the water, use a light wash of ultramarine, and drop in thicker paint immediately. There's water in the first blue wash so don't dilute the second coat too much or the final colour will be too weak.

THE RIGGER

The rigger is a delightful brush with a long delicate point, so named because in the old days it was used for putting in the rigging on pictures of sailing ships. The length makes it much more flexible and versatile, than ordinary round brushes, particularly when held right at the end of the handle. Its long hair means that with practice, you can get strokes from a mere hair line to 5mm (¼in) wide, depending on the pressure exerted. It is very good for figures in landscapes, winter trees (which I make my students practise over and over again), and grasses. I have to say that to control it properly and get the best out of the rigger, it does take practice, but it really will repay all your efforts.

I find that so many students spoil their winter scenes by poorly drawn branches – which let the whole painting down. Remember, a painting is only as good as its worst bit!

The trick is to get the tapering of the branches from the trunk to the tips of the twigs. At first you'll find that you'll get branches like hose pipes, or what I call 6m (20ft) high twigs. I've also seen many trunks with whiskers! However, don't despair, things will quickly improve with practice, and you'll soon be producing convincing trees.

With regard to small figures, you hold the brush further down in the more conventional way, but we will talk about this later, in the section on People and Animals on page 114.

When drawing figures, hold the brush down towards the ferrule to give lighter control. The different thicknesses are obtained by varying the weight on the brush.

With the rigger you can get enormous differences of thickness by pressing really hard, and gradually releasing the pressure until, at the end of the stroke, you flick it off the paper in an arc.

When painting grasses and undergrowth the brush is held at the very top, and again just flick the brush off the paper in an arc. Don't use the brush too dry.

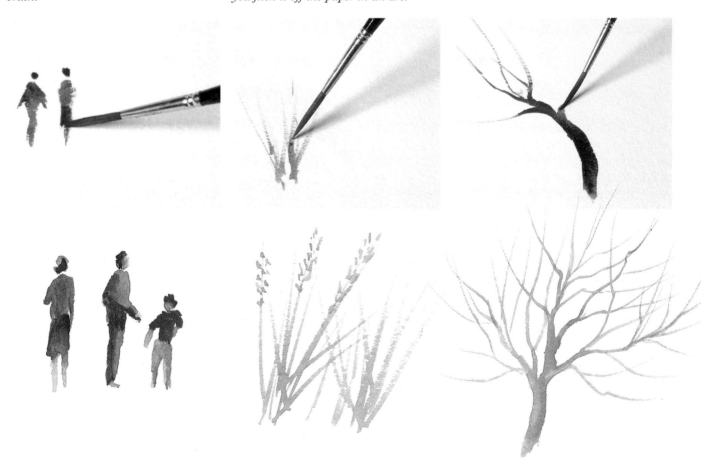

Practice

The seven vignettes on the next three pages are designed specifically to improve your skills with each of the brushes, and will show you how they combine to produce a complete painting. Each brush has its own particular use, and will do its own job perfectly once the techniques have been learned.

For your own practice copy these seven pictures, using the appropriate brushes. Don't try to copy them meticulously, but try to use as few strokes as possible. The most important thing is to keep the freshness and spontaneity, so vital for a successful watercolour.

This scene uses all three main brushes. The background of this tiny snow scene is a mixture of light red and ultramarine with some rigger work added while still wet. The warm colours of the foliage are a mixture of raw sienna and light red. Those in the background are dropped into the still-damp wash, and the nearer ones are done on dry paper. The stream is a mixture of light red and ultramarine. The fence is done with the edge of the 1in flat brush.

For the harbour scene, you'll mostly need the 1in flat and the hake, and the colours are ultramarine, burnt umber and lemon yellow. Paint the background in with a weak mixture of ultramarine and burnt umber using the 1in flat, and drawing round the buildings as you go.

The dock itself has a lot of varying colours to make it interesting, and you'll need to paint it in very quickly, again using the 1in flat. Notice how I've got the white boat too, by simply painting round it. You can add the masts, posts and warehouse roof by touching in lightly with the edge of the 1in flat.

This is done using the hake and the rigger only. Starting from the back, paint in the distant woods with a pale bluey wash. Then add warmer, thicker paint while the wash is still wet, so bringing the picture forward, plane by plane. The colours are ultramarine, raw sienna and burnt umber. The rigger work should be done when the first washes are dry, and the foreground tree should be put in with the back of the hake.

This is an autumn scene, and the colours should be raw sienna, light red, ultramarine and burnt umber. Put the background trees in with a mixture of ultramarine and light red, and add an occasional area of raw sienna to give variety. You'll get the right effect for the distant banks with raw sienna, and a touch of light red.

Next do the lake. Wet this over completely with pale blue and make downward strokes with the distant tree colour into the original damp wash. The streak must be taken out immediately with a dry hake. The foreground trees and ground are painted in richer paint using burnt umber, light red and raw sienna, adding the calligraphy with the rigger and judicious use of the fingernail.

For this rocky seascape, you'll need the hake and the 1in flat. Put the sea in with the hake, in a mixture of ultramarine and a little light red, leaving areas of white paper for the waves. Use the 1in flat to put in the rocks. The foreground needs to be put in very quickly with the hake to obtain a spontaneous dry-brush effect, using very light pressure. The rich green of the tree is mixed from paynes grey and lemon yellow.

The background woods should be painted in first with a weak mixture of light red, ultramarine and raw sienna, adding a few strokes with the rigger for distant trees. Using stronger paint, put in the nearer trees with the hake using fingernails and the rigger on top. The foreground shadows are a mixture of ultramarine, light red and raw sienna. Finally I added a man and his dog with the rigger.

Techniques

We looked in the last chapter at the different strokes you can make with the three brushes, to give variety, and to help indicate subjects and surfaces. We should now discuss more fully the various techniques that are based around the proportion of water to paint to use and the amount of pressure to put on the brushes. The combination of these two factors will enable you to produce a great variety of effects quite easily.

Simplest of all is a straightforward wash, which can be put on with the hake or the 1in flat. By thinning the paint with water, you can get a wash; as delicate as a whisper. This does not mean using a saturated brush that immediately leaves you out of control. Once you have mixed the paint with plenty

of water, a touch of the brush on your paint rag will not change the intended tone, but will get rid of excess moisture. This will allow you to soften a delicate wash while still remaining in control. Alternatively, you can make a wash that has a high paint content, which will be richer, darker or more brilliant in colour.

The second technique is traditionally called wet into wet. This is something of a misnomer, and leads to a lot of anguish for beginners. Basically, the process is to put a wettish wash on the paper, dry your brush and make a very rich, sometimes neat mixture of paint, and apply this immediately while the first wash is still damp. You must remember that water is already on the paper when you apply the

When you are laying a wash you should try and put it on lightly and clearly but don't go backwards and forwards or it will not look transparent. The less you disturb the surface of the paper the better. The secret is to get the right tone first time without altering it. Always have a scrap handy for trial efforts.

For wet into wet, first put on a weak wash of ultramarine mixed with a touch of lemon yellow. While this is still wet, put on a strong, rich, almost neat mixture of lemon yellow and paynes grey. It may seem too strong, but once it's over the first damp wash, it will soften and diffuse in a few seconds, but will not run away. The secret is not to leave the first wash too long before putting in the second, and don't make the second wash too weak.

It will take a lot of practice, but you'll get it right eventually and find that it will all be worthwhile. To get the profile of the trees you'll need to use the corner of the hake, stroking downwards, rather than using the flat edge.

Dry-brush effect is created by skimming over the high points of the paper and leaving the hollows bare. The brush need not necessarily be dry but the knack is to brush it over the paper very lightly and very quickly. Much depends on the roughness of the paper itself.

second layer, hence the need now for very little or no water. If this is done correctly you will have a beautiful, rich effect which is also soft.

The third technique is known as dry brush. Again the description is not entirely accurate. The effect you're striving for is a quality of texture in which the paper itself shows through. The secret here is to stroke the brush across the paper extremely lightly and quickly. This action will get the effect irrespective of the amount of water in the paint. In other words, the brush itself doesn't actually need to be dry!

Lastly, there's calligraphy, which should always be delicate and flowing. It is essential that you learn to control the rigger with confidence for this.

This simple illustration shows how the various techniques can be combined. First of all the sky. This you must paint wet into wet by putting on a very pale wash of raw sienna, and immediately painting round the clouds with strongish ultramarine which will quickly diffuse and give the effect shown. When this is dry, wash in the hillsides making them stronger and warmer as they come forward.

The trees at their base can be added in stronger paint before the wash is dry. Put in the river with a quick wash of blue to match the sky, dropping in some of the colour from the hills behind. Finally, try your dry brush technique for the foreshore using swift, light strokes of the hake, afterwards adding the foreground bracken.

On these two pages are more examples showing the use of the various techniques. In the painting on the left the distant hill is put in using a weak mixture of ultramarine and light red. The autumn trees are a mixture of light red and raw sienna added before the hillside is dry, still using the hake.

The foreground bush and bank are put in with the dry brush, while the posts can be added with single touches of the edge of the 1in flat. For the grasses you'll need delicate strokes of the rigger, while you can try flicks of the fingernail in the bush.

Above is a fast-moving river. Start with the wet into wet background. First put in a weak blue wash over the tree area, then add some dark green made from lemon yellow and paynes grey, and let it diffuse to get the effect of distance. When this is dry, put in the right-hand bank in a warmer green to bring it forward (by using more yellow). The rocks on both sides of the picture can be put in very quickly and simply with directional strokes of the hake.

Now put in the river using dry brush, leaving much of the water as untouched white paper. Finally add the calligraphy with the rigger. Again, you can use your fingernail while the paint is damp, but with discretion.

On the left is a simple estuary scene. Paint the sky with a very weak wash of raw sienna followed by a graduated wash of ultramarine while the raw sienna is still wet. When this is dry, paint in the distant hill and add the trees using wet into wet. The water you should try to put in with only one or two strokes of the 1in flat.

Now we come to the foreground. Here you'll need mostly dry brush, built up first with quick horizontal strokes to provide plenty of sparkle, with some vertical strokes in strong paint for the bush etc. The large rock can be painted in with rich paint, and you can do as I did and use a credit card to scrape off the top.

Finally the little yacht can be added by making a mask from two pieces of overlapping paper and removing the paint between them with a damp rag. Add the grasses with flicks of the rigger.

What you need to do is to use some of each of these techniques in your painting. For instance, just to use wet into wet in a picture would be the same as having an orchestra consisting entirely of violins. It would be dull and incomplete.

As you can see, they all have their strengths and weaknesses. The wash is the best way to indicate shapes. Simplicity is the keynote, but too much will become monotonous. Wet into wet is very exciting and satisfying, but used all over a painting will make everything vague and woolly. Dry brush, too, is spontaneous and gives great sparkle, but must be used with restraint. Calligraphy is decorative and descriptive, but can be very fussy if overdone. Used together, however, they will provide a satisfying and entertaining painting.

LIGHT OUT OF DARK

Part of the mystique of watercolour, and the reason why a lot of people are afraid to try it, is this belief that once the paint is on the paper, there's no way of altering it. This of course is ridiculous, and I will show you some of the ways of removing paint from your paper. I often find that people, having done a good painting, then spoil it by over-working the foreground. I've done it myself many times. A damp rag along with a strong nerve will remove the over-worked mud in seconds, leaving a tinted area that makes an ideal base for more judicious and economic texture after it's dry. Different makes of paper do respond in different ways. One thing always to remember, is never to alter anything while the paper is still damp, as this is the dangerous time. Wait until the paper is bone dry. Another area which sometimes goes wrong is the sky. If you don't mix the blue properly, you can get ugly patches, but these too can be removed when dry with a judicious

amount of spit on your handkerchief! Practice this first on a discarded painting.

Now let's get down to more specific techniques. The hog's hair brush shown on page 12, normally used for oil painting, can be used with clean water and a clean rag to dab gently but firmly, to remove small areas of paint or to soften edges, such as on waves. Again, practise this on discarded paintings. It can be used effectively with a sheet of paper as a mask, to straighten horizons, or with two pieces of paper, for example to make light masts or even distant sailboats.

Another device I use is to press my knuckle into damp paint, especially on the foreground, to obtain texture. Also, a fingernail will create distant light tree trunks or foreground grasses. These methods should be used with discretion and economy, as used indiscriminately they look cheap and nasty.

Another way of removing damp paint, especially from the tops of rocks, is to use an old credit card,

This shows the use of the hog's hair brush to soften and remove paint in small areas. You can adapt this method to create a soft moon by using it in conjunction with blotting paper.

This shows the use of the credit card to remove paint on the top surface of rocks while the paint is still damp.

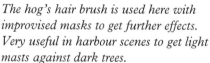

The hog's hair brush is used here with improvised masks to get further effects. Very useful in harbour scenes to get light masts against dark trees.

This time the hake is used previously dried on a clean rag to get the effect of a patch of light on water. Two patches on a lake at different distances is enough.

The Stanley knife blade is used here delicately, after the paint is dry, to indicate distant masts, grasses and possibly even seagulls!

Here we have the effect of a knuckle used in damp paint. It's useful in foregrounds to provide texture to break up an otherwise boring wash.

or part of it. One of my favourite ways of getting a streak on the water where a slight breeze has disturbed the normally calm surface, is to use my hake dried on a rag to make it thirsty. I then sweep it across the surface horizontally using the edge. You'll see many examples of this on other pages. It is done while the surface is still damp. A Stanley knife blade is useful for putting in light grasses, white birds, or to correct blemishes. This must be done on a dry surface with great delicacy of touch, as you could easily destroy the surface of the paper, leaving a nasty mark.

In this picture you will see some of the effects shown below. The hog's hair brush is used to pick out the setting sun – a much more natural effect than trying to mask it out. The fingernail is worked into wet paint for the trunk of the tree and grasses with a little use of the knuckles to create texture.

Here the seagulls are picked out with a Stanley knife blade while the yachts on the far horizon are done by forming a mask with two pieces of paper and rubbing with a hog's hair brush. The horizon can be lightened by turning the painting upside down and scrubbing lightly with the hog's hair brush against a sheet of paper.

The credit card has been used on the top of the rocks. The grasses can be done either while still damp with a fingernail or wet with a Stanley knife.

Practice

I would now like you to practise all the brush strokes and techniques by doing three paintings. They are designed to employ all the brushes in various ways, as well as different water content. It is a good idea to set yourself a time limit, (perhaps you should use a kitchen timer) of say 15 minutes, so that you'll avoid over-working. Remember that a quick stroke will be more exciting than a slow one, and I want you to be as economical with the strokes as possible – rather like a golfer! Don't be afraid to leave the white paper where appropriate or to use good, rich paint where required. Remember that timidity is very often your worst enemy.

This gentle snow scene is done very much wet into wet using just three colours: ultramarine, light red and burnt umber. Start off very weakly at the back with blue, gradually strengthening it with light red and burnt umber as you work forward. Use your fingernail or the top of your brush to get the light trees, combined with the rigger for the dark trees, all mixed up with the wet into wet colour – this could be very exciting to do.

Finally do the water and its reflections. Use a pale blue with light red, and while this is still wet, using a dry hake, wipe two horizontal strokes to create the sheen on the river where the breeze has ruffled the water.

Right, put the sea in first with a mixture of ultramarine and a tiny touch of yellow, leaving plenty of white paper for the surf. Now tackle the rocks using the hake and 1in flat. The tops of the rocks can be burnt umber and raw sienna, the side light red and ultramarine.

The pale yellowy-green grass should counterchange against the dark tree, the colour of which is made from paynes grey and lemon yellow used strongly and richly, but applied by dancing over the paper lightly with the hake. To prevent it from looking muddy, apply only one layer of paint.

Above is a snow scene showing a quarry face. Paint the background trees wet into wet using weak ultramarine together with a stronger burnt umber. The rock face gives you an ideal opportunity to practise your dry brush, combined with some wet into wet. Use mainly blue and burnt umber for this, trying to get plenty of sparkle and texture. You can't paint this carefully. It has to be done with vigour and courage to make it exciting. The cracks in the rock and grasses can be added at the end with the rigger.

Tonal Values

This chapter is probably the most important in the book, so do be patient and stay with me. First let me explain what tonal values are. They are the range of lightness to darkness of any colour. It's probably easier to think of a numbered scale going from 1-100. For instance, the pure white of the paper would be 1 while solid black would be classed as 100.

Beginners are often scared of each end of the range. They're afraid of leaving white paper and of committing themselves to a really strong dark. They stay in their own little comfort zone around 50. The result of this is weak, flat, boring pictures with no sparkle – rather like someone playing a piano only using the middle octave.

To get sparkle and excitement into your pictures, you'll need to contrast adjacent areas of tones, such as putting 80 against 20, or the most stimulating of all, 1 against 100. Tackle this aspect of tonal values first, working in only one colour and creating a wide range of tones from very light to very dark. This is the quickest way of learning about tonal values, and will show you how pictures should be made up of lights and darks in the areas of greatest interest, with mid-tones in the supporting areas and background. If you learn to do this skilfully, you will quickly be able to organize your paintings tonally, thereby creating an overall sense of design. I should stress that you will never be a good artist in any medium unless you understand tonal values.

In doing these sketches, forget about details completely and reduce the subject to a pattern of lights and darks. This leads on to another very important aspect: counterchange, or the deliberate placing of light objects dark, and dark against light. Of course this occurs in real life, but you'll often have to exaggerate it throughout the picture to produce the necessary effect. Artists have been doing this for hundreds of years. Look at the paintings in this section and see how I've tried to practise what I preach!

In the three pictures on this page, the painting has been reduced almost to abstract patterns, and it's the juxtapositioning which gives the viewer a clue to what is happening. If the pattern itself is strong and contrasting enough, then this is sufficient.

In the simple coastal scene on the left much has been left to the viewer's imagination. This could be either a river flowing into the sea, or a coastal road behind a rocky shore. The strongest values have been kept to the front, where I've counterchanged the light wall against a dark tree. The two hills in the background are separated only by a faint tonal difference. The odd patch of untouched paper adds sparkle, while the horizontal shape of the rocks balance up the tree.

In the sketch on the left, the white paper says foam, the black rocks, and even the two tones in the foreground say wet and dry sand.

On the left we have a strong pattern of lights and darks. The soft background shape of the hill contrasts well against the sharp filigree of the bridge, which because it's light against dark provides the main focal point. The lines of the water, too, point to the bridge, again showing how little detail is needed if the pattern is right. Note too the checkerboard pattern of the dark rocks against the untouched paper, which gives counterchange and so adds excitement.

Besides the full range of tones from 1-100, one of the most dramatic things about the picture on the right is the directional flow of the brush strokes, and the strong feeling of texture from the wet-into-wet distant trees, to the dry brush using completely neat paint. This is a very good exercise in dry brush, so why not try it.

These tonal sketches can be done in soft pencil and be very small – almost postage-stamp size, but I prefer, and I think you'll find it easier, to do them in burnt umber, perhaps with the 1in flat, although still keeping them quite small – about 7.5 x 10cm (3-4in) in size. At this scale and using this brush it is impossible to get too detailed, and you're forced to simplify the picture into a range of different lights, darks and mid-tones.

This is also a very good exercise in using your paint. For example, leave the white paper for your highlights and learn to obtain the rest of the range by changing the water content. To get the darkest dark you need hardly any water at all. Perhaps the most difficult thing to do is to create a particular tone first time and avoid altering it, which would give a muddy result.

This of course needs practice, and just as a musician has to practise his scales continuously to avoid playing a wrong note in performance, you'll find that the more you practise your tonal sketches, the fresher your paintings will be. After all, you wouldn't start a building by simply buying a pile of bricks, you'd just get a proper design. So many large expensive pieces of paper have been ruined by a lack of preparation.

Although this seems obvious, I have enormous difficulty in persuading my own students that this is so, and as I've said, most of them want to plunge blindly into a painting without so much as giving a thought to its content. They seem to regard the tonal sketch as a waste of time and paper, but I hope that by now you're convinced that it is a valuable aid to doing a good painting.

This is all very well, but you're probably saying to yourself, this is fine with one colour, but what happens when you try to convert your tonal sketch into a full colour painting. As we said at the beginning, tone is the lightness or darkness of any colour. For example if you painted a red house against a green tree, and the two colours, although different hues were similar in tone, the overall effect would be flat. It would be necessary to make the tree a darker green or the house a lighter red. What I'm saying is that a full colour painting should still "read" well tonally.

Here we have the same scene using a full range of tonal values from about 5 for the sea to 100 for the foreground tree. The distant cliffs are painted lightly, in subtle tones to give depth, while the foreground is full of contrast, sparkle and texture. Note how the dry brush has added to the textural quality. Also, the lightest light has been used against the darkest dark, creating a strong contrast that draws the eye and makes the foreground tree the focal point.

This is an example of what happens when the various tones come too close together, with insufficient contrast between adjacent objects. The scene looks flat and dull and the forms are not clearly distinguishable.

This is a common fault among beginners, who are often afraid to leave the white paper to speak for itself, or to use rich dark paint. They always seem to add too much water, which results in paintings like this.

The sketch above shows the effective use of counterchange. Notice how the sails on the ship have been painted dark against the sky, and then graduated so that they appear light against the mid-tone of the distant shore. The moored dinghies are counterchanged against each other, creating a checkerboard pattern. The distant houses are also counterchanged against the trees, but with much less contrast because of the distance.

On the left the scene is divided into three separate depths. The far right-hand shore is kept as a single weak tone. The nearer shore on the left is slightly more contrasting, whilst the main punch and sparkle is reserved for the front part of the picture where I've often used 1 against 100, making it very dramatic. Notice too, how important the directional strokes are, which help to take the eye into the picture. I used the 1in flat for the distant shores, yacht and landing stage, and the hake for the rest of the picture with judicious use of the fingernail.

AERIAL PERSPECTIVE

If you're going to create the effect of a scene, which may go back miles, on a small flat sheet of paper, you have to resort to artistic tricks. One way is to exaggerate the effect of aerial perspective. This has nothing to do with linear perspective, which is the effect of lines running to a vanishing point on the horizon. It is to do with the principle in nature, that light tones appear to recede into the distance whereas darker tones seem to come forward. My way of describing this is that you must whisper in the background and shout in the foreground. In terms of a tonal range of 1-100, background hills may be 10-15, while a foreground object right at the front of the picture might be 100. At first it may be difficult when you see an obviously dark tree on the horizon, to restrain yourself and not give it what you think is its true value. However, instead you must deliberately tone down its value, otherwise you'll have no power left for the foreground.

I always start from the back and work forward, moving in planes, increasing in strength until I get to the front of the picture. Also, distant objects should be flattened, for instance a distant wood or even a single tree would have no moulding on it at all, but would be treated as a simple flat wash.

Up to this point, I've been talking about getting effects in one colour, but when it comes to full colour, aerial perspective is taken a stage further. The more the picture recedes into the distance, the cooler and bluer the colours get, whereas the further forward, the richer and warmer they become.

This painting is a good example of aerial perspective because the scene goes back a good mile. You'll need only four colours to do this: ultramarine, raw sienna, paynes grey and lemon yellow. First paint the sky by putting on a very pale wash of raw sienna. While it is still wet, lay in a stronger wash of ultramarine, gradually taking the pressure off the brush as you work down towards the horizon. Now use a very weak wash of ultramarine and yellow for the distant hills, strengthening it on the right as it comes forward.

Put in the two distant groups of trees using the wet into wet technique, and gradually move forward, warming up the green with more yellow. The front tree on the right should be painted in a strong mixture of lemon yellow and paynes grey. Paint the reflections in the river, again using wet into wet.

Practice

On these two pages there are four tonal sketches. I would like you to use them as a basis for your own paintings. First copy them directly in burnt umber, then close the book and convert your sketches into larger colour paintings. It's essential that you keep the tones the right strength irrespective of the colour, so that if you made a photocopy of them afterwards, they would still "read" well. It's so easy to weaken the whole picture and make it too flat when you start to use colour.

The scene above is all about texture and counterchange. Notice how the dark trees behind pick out the white cottages. There's plenty of opportunity here to use a dry-brush hake on top of quick horizontal strokes. The windows and posts will be best done with the 1in flat.

Right, keep the distant hills in cool colours, pale blue or even mauve, which means adding a touch of light red to the blue. Gradually warm each layer of ground as it comes forward by using more yellow or raw sienna. Make the river flow by using quick brush strokes.

The back of the scene above is very much wet into wet, so you'll need to use cooler blue/grey colours at the back of the woods, and warmer colours at the front. These colours of course should reflect in the water, as should any light trunks you make. You can use warm raw sienna for the foliage showing through the snow, and any shadows should be done in pale blue.

The picture on the right will help you to learn how to use directional strokes with the hake. First use the edges and corners to make the fir trees, along with a fingernail for the light trunks. You could paint the distant banks with sloping strokes and try to sweep the brush quickly in an arc to get the sweep of the beach. Be careful to leave the boat as white paper, and add a little dry-brush texture here and there.

Composition

Having studied the last chapter you are now, in musical terms, conversant with the scales. So it's time to move on to composition. In other words, it's time to learn how to design the picture, using all the tones to create a cohesive and unified whole.

In America, I'm often asked to judge art shows. The main object is to reduce perhaps 250 entries to about 100 that will actually be exhibited. No matter in what medium, or what techniques have been used, the overall criteria that a judge uses to select or reject a painting, is whether it is well designed. So many pictures lack unity and simply don't hang together. It doesn't matter how well painted the various elements are, if they don't balance each other to create a harmonious whole it is not a well-designed painting. Many of the painters know all about the theory of design, but once they start painting and struggling with the medium itself, all thoughts of organizing the composition are forgotten and they end up with a fragmented picture. Much has been written about the "Principles of Design", which is a help if you can remember them all when you're out in the countryside. What I want to do here is just to give you a few simple and easily digestible rules.

The very first point is that you must have a very clear objective. In other words you must know what

The main object of interest here is the white rowing boat, because it's the lightest light against the darkest dark. Both the figure on the quay and the distant sail boat are of secondary interest, as the degree of contrast is much lower. Notice how the distant shoreline is played down to give distance, and this is helped by the lack of detail. The strong contrasting texture in the foreground is used to bring it forward.

Three devices have been used here to make the hut the main object of interest. First the light roof, which has been left as pure paper, is counterchanged against the dark trees behind it. It's also the area of greatest detail, and finally the eye is taken in to the picture along the river to finish up at the hut. A vertical element (in what is generally a horizontal picture) is provided by the foreground trees, which also balance the mass on the other side.

your painting is about. It's no good just painting aimlessly. What was it that stopped you in your tracks and made you want to paint this particular scene in the first place? This is vitally important, so keep it in your mind. It will lead to the next thing - where to put your centre of interest, which is the focal point of the whole painting. Don't let yourself be distracted from this by anything else. Whatever it was that you first saw, be it a hut, figure or boat, must be more important than anything else in the finished painting.

Where in the picture do we put this element so that it attracts the viewer's attention first? In fact it's easier to tell you where *not* to put it. Never in the centre of the paper or right on the edge. Ideally it should be in a spot where the distance from all four edges is different.

The next point to think about is how to attract the viewer's attention to it. Perhaps it would be the brightest spot of colour, or the most detailed object, or the area of biggest contrast, that is, the lightest light against the darkest dark, as we learned in the previous chapter. However, there are also devices we can use to point at our object. It could be the curve of a river, the direction of a boat or even converging lines of trees.

The eye is always drawn to figures and man-made objects in a landscape, and here we have the two elements together, forming a single centre of interest. The dark figures are in shadow and are silhouetted against the light background for impact, while the building is in full sunlight. The two are further linked by the foreground tree. The lane itself issues an invitation into the painting, helped by the directional strokes of the brush.

Another rule we have to learn is how to balance a painting between main and subsidiary areas, and the easiest way is to think of a see-saw. Not however as two equal objects on each side of the picture; that would be very boring and is called formal balance. Informal balance is much better, such as a large shape towards the centre of a picture being balanced by smaller shapes away from the centre.

Probably the most important point of all, however, is to create unity in a painting through the way the different elements are combined, using balance, tonal contrasts, colour harmony, pattern and the echoing of shapes and colours. You can tell at once if a painting does not hang together, because rather like a misspelled word, it will jump out at you. This is the main purpose of all these tonal sketches. Even though they're only the size of postage stamps, they'll immediately tell you if you've gone wrong, and you'll

avoid wasting an expensive sheet of watercolour paper.

To get back to that all important tonal sketch, you may need three or four attempts to make sure you've got the best possible composition. It doesn't matter how small these are or how fast you do them, they'll still show up any design errors. Look at your sketch very critically and once you're satisfied, you can start your painting with much more confidence, and you'll be free to concentrate on actually handling the paint. One of the greatest dangers lies in allowing yourself to stray from your original and well-designed tonal sketch. If you do this, you'll finish up with a pale and unsatisfactory version, lacking the punch and unity of the sketch.

Finally, another good point to remember, is that an artist is an entertainer and as such has a responsibility not to bore his or her viewers, but to interest and entertain them.

A simple but classic composition where the eye is taken into the picture by the curve in the foreground, round the rocks and onto the yacht, the main object of interest. Notice how the dark foreground trees are balanced by the clouds in the right of the picture. The dark trees are counterchanged against the rocks and how the background trees are much lighter, giving depth to the painting.

The human figure always attracts attention. Being the main object of interest, it is placed just off centre. The sunlit houses are of secondary interest and are counterchanged against the distant foliage. The curve of the river takes the eye to the figure, which is in turn counterchanged against a light background. Notice the tonal difference between the further and nearer trees.

Practice

Now's your chance to put into practice all you've learned in the previous pages about composition. Use this knowledge to alter the pictures on these two pages. Each presents new problems to solve. The first three are tonal sketches and all have things wrong with them, and must be improved by changing the composition and adding elements of your own. Once you've done this and are satisfied, then try changing them into colour paintings, but at the same time, try to retain the basic tonal values.

Both colour paintings are good basic compositions, but I've left you lots of room to add your own ideas and change things around to suit yourself. Yet another challenge would be to change the proportions, particularly in the larger painting.

Take great care and thought over these exercises, trying several possibilities in each case. In all these compositions, remember to keep your foregrounds strong and contrasting, and the backgrounds flatter and less detailed.

This tonal sketch of a coastal scene is a little too top heavy, the weight being too much on the right. Try to add something on the left to balance it better. It could be another tree, a large rock or a figure coming up the hill. You could also lower the horizon so that you would see more sky.

The main fault in this composition is that the tree, which is the chief object of interest, is right in the middle. Always a mistake! Try re-arranging the picture using the same elements of foreground, rock, tree, fences etc., to improve it. You could add more weight to the tree by giving it summer foliage.

This composition with its S-shaped river is quite reasonable, but would be greatly improved by the addition of a vertical element, and a main object of interest. You could add a hut or a figure or a foreground tree.

Here we have a scene consisting of three separate depths, the distant hills being seen through a gap in the trees and over a cornfield. The trees are reflected in the pond. Try changing this composition by introducing a foreground tree on the right to balance the mass on the left, or introduce a standing fisherman or even a boat. You could first draw the figures on tracing paper and move them around your painting until you find the best position. Another thing you could do is to change the pond into a river, flowing through the break in the trees.

Here we have an unusually square format with the composition leading the eye into the picture towards the main object of interest, the sunlit distant buildings. The main vertical element is the foreground tree, which is balanced by the dark hedge on the left. Bearing this in mind, use the same elements in different ways. For instance, change the format to a proportionately wider one, perhaps putting an S-bend into the road.

To make the scene completely different, change it to a snow scene, with winter trees, snow on the roofs and converging tracks in the snow emphasized by the shadows, which would be pale blue. Now try reversing the picture left to right, and perhaps adding a figure at the end of the road to provide an additional element.

Colour

Like everyone else, I started off by buying about 20 colours, thinking that having a colour for every purpose would make life easier. It didn't of course! Faced with rows of different colours, it was difficult to decide, for instance, which blue to use, especially in the open air. I felt like an accordionist with 120 little buttons to press and not being sure what they'd produce. However, I gradually reduced the number to seven, and soon felt at home with them and came to know them intimately.

Many people might think that a larger range would surely be needed in sunnier climes. However, colours out of the tube are quite bright, and in countries with cooler, wetter climates they need to be "greyed off" to reflect the colours seen in the landscape. For instance brown must be introduced to the blue. Warmer colours too, are not quite as warm and will have to be modified to get the subtle shades of the countryside. However, in warmer countries there's no need for this mellowing effect, and the colours can be used straight out of the tube.

I make no apology for repeating myself when I say

Lemon Yellow *This colour varies a lot depending on the make. With some brands lemon yellow is the brightest of bright yellows, yet in other makes it is an opaque, creamy yellow. Get the brightest yellow you can. If this is not the lemon yellow, probably cadmium yellow pale is the safest. You'll find you need twice as much of lemon yellow as any other colour.*

More water

With alizarin

Raw Sienna *This is an earth colour, and one of the oldest ever made. I use it in nearly every painting I do. It's similar to yellow ochre, but is much more transparent.*

More water

With light red

Ultramarine *My only blue. I know there are many others such as cobalt or cerulean, but I think you will find that ultramarine will carry you through most situations. It's a little crude when used raw, so I always temper it with other colours.*

More water

With alizarin

that it's false economy to be mean with your paints. It's only by using rich paint that you'll get the power and freedom to create exciting pictures. To sum up then, my suggestion is to use few colours, but plenty of it, and a lot less water than most of my students, who seem to use too much water and not enough paint, resulting in weak, washed-out paintings. I can always tell just by looking at a student's palette whether the painting is going to be rich or weak.

In the accompanying illustrations, I'm going to show you the various permutations of my seven colours. It's vital that you become so familiar with these that you can use them almost from instinct. With practice you'll get to a stage when you'll know without thinking about it, how to get a certain shade of blue or grey, and you'll be able to concentrate your mind entirely on the subject in front of you.

It is appropriate now to mention about warm and cool colours. Warm colours are those which contain red, orange, yellow or brown, and cool colours are those with blue in them. They can all be used to create distance in your painting. More of this later.

With ultramarine   *With paynes grey*

With alizarin   *With paynes grey*

Here we have paynes grey and raw sienna. The hills in the background are watered-down paynes grey, while the nearer hill is paynes grey and raw sienna to make a warmer colour. The foreground is raw sienna and the trees are a stronger mix of the two colours.

With burnt umber   *With paynes grey*

The winter scene is painted with light red, ultramarine and raw sienna. The background hill is weak ultramarine. The foreground trees are a mixture of ultramarine and light red, with touches of raw sienna.

Light Red *Like raw sienna, this is also an earth colour. It's very strong and can swamp other colours, so use it sparingly. However, it looks great mixed with raw sienna for Mediterranean roofs. With ultramarine it will make beautifully transparent shadows.*

More water   *With ultramarine*

Alizarin Crimson *Unlike the yellow, you'll find a tube of this lasts a long time. It's a very cool, intense red. Use it with discretion. I use it mainly with paynes grey for clouds.*

More water   *With burnt umber*

Burnt Umber *Another colour made from ground earth. I always use it to make my tonal sketches. Mixed with ultramarine it produces a whole range of interesting greys.*

More water   *With lemon yellow*

Paynes Grey *This is regarded by some people as the black sheep in my palette and is often frowned upon. It's tremendously useful, but never use it by itself. It should always be tempered by other colours. Used with yellow it makes great greens. Remember that it always dries lighter than it appears when wet.*

More water   *With light red*

With alizarin

With burnt umber

With paynes grey

With ultramarine

The mountains are painted in light red and ultramarine. While this is still wet, add pure raw sienna for the trees. Weak raw sienna is used for the foreground bank.

With raw sienna

With paynes grey

There are only two colours in this little snow scene - burnt umber and ultramarine. Weak ultramarine is used for the mountains with a little burnt umber to calm it down. The shadows are ultramarine and the trees are made up with rich burnt umber and a touch of blue.

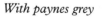

With lemon yellow

With raw sienna

The two colours here are paynes grey and lemon yellow. The two colours are mixed with varying amounts of water to produce this sketch. Starting from the back with pure paynes grey, the lemon yellow is added as we come further forward, with the trees being made up of a stronger mix of the two colours.

GREENS

I hate ready-made greens. Some of them remind me more of disinfectant than foliage, so I mix them all myself. The thought of mixing various greens seems to frighten many people, but once you've acquired a little basic knowledge, it can become a real pleasure. After all, so much of the landscape around us is composed of greens, it really is impossible to avoid them.

The most obvious danger is to make them weak, watery and monotonous, so that they become the ruination of many landscapes. Students seem to find a rich, dark foreground green the most difficult colour to mix, but only because again, they put too much water with it.

In this picture you'll see how warm and cool greens are used to create depth, so that the viewer feels that they could actually walk into the wood. When painting this scene, the coolest blue-green is washed over the complete width, and much stronger, richer greens are added into the first wash, while it is still wet.

The distant trees are also added at this stage so that they diffuse, while the light foreground trees are scraped out of the rich greens. The light foreground grass is counterchanged against the dark at the base of the woods. The path is painted in a very weak light red and when this is dry, the shadows are added with a mixture of light red and ultramarine.

As you'll see from the illustrations below, you can get a huge range of greens by using just three colours and varying amounts of water. If you copy the combinations opposite over and over again, this will improve your skills no end. Another thing which might help is to pick leaves of varying colours and try to match them with paint. You'll probably find that the colours range from a very blue green right through to a very yellow green.

Another good exercise is to study the difference in greens between, say, vertical trees and horizontal grass. You'll find that the grass facing the light is always yellower and lighter than the trees, but I've often seen them painted exactly the same colour.

DO'S AND DONT'S

Do keep your distant greens weak.

Do make your foreground greens rich.

Do practice mixing the greens until you can produce a particular green instantly.

Don't make your greens muddy, by painting over and over again.

Don't use too much water.

Don't forget to counterchange light greens against dark greens.

These are the distant greens, where the proportion of water is higher. On the left we have mainly blue with just a touch of lemon yellow. The centre and right-hand examples contain progressively more lemon yellow and less water.

Now we come to the middle-distance greens. Again the proportion of yellow increases from the left and less water is used. On the right you'll see what is probably the brightest green you can get. It's almost yellow with just a touch of blue. You'll need plenty of yellow for these, to prevent them from looking washed out.

Here we have the really rich dark greens which are used in foregrounds. To achieve these, ignore the blue and just add paynes grey progressively to the yellow. If you use too much water, you'll never get these greens first time off, and if you use more than one wash, the colour will become muddy.

COLOUR AND DISTANCE

The artist has to cheat a bit in order to create the illusion of distance in the scene he is painting on a flat piece of paper, a scene which may be receding a mile or more. There are two main ways of doing this. One is, as we've already learned, just by using tone. The other is by using cool and warm colours. In most cases the two devices are used together. My own way of putting it is, that you must whisper in the background and shout in the foreground.

A third device, which you'll see used in the accompanying picture, is not to use any detail at all in the distance, just flat washes with no shading or form, relying on the profiles to describe the landscape. Only when you reach the foreground can you let yourself go with rich colour, texture detail and lots of contrast. This doesn't mean that all foregrounds should be dark. Use lots of counterchange as in the picture on the right. Notice how the tiny, dark green fir trees are silhouetted against a lighter patch behind. You will also notice light grasses against dark. There will be a tremendous difference in the ratio of water to paint in any one picture. I usually find that I use a high water content at the back of a painting, but by the time I get to the foreground, I'm using lots of strong, rich almost neat colour.

Below are spectrums of colours which are used to give the illusion of distance. The top line consists of summer colours, which are described on the previous page, and begin on the left with cool, diluted tints for the distance, graduating to rich, juicy colour in the foreground.

Underneath we have autumn colours. In the distance you would use the weak mauve made from light red and ultramarine, graduating through to the rich warm browns in the foreground. You'll see the various colours used in the large picture on this page.

In this soft, misty, Irish scene there's a great feeling of space and distance. The distant hills have been painted in first in soft and subdued grey-greens against a graduated sky. As the scene comes forward, the colours are warmed and strengthened, culminating in the rich and contrasting foreground.

The foreground colours are raw sienna warmed slightly with light red, while the greens are used at full strength mixed from lemon yellow and paynes grey. All texture has been confined to this area and less and less detail is used as the picture recedes, which is yet another way of indicating depth.

Practice

With these four pictures don't just copy them, try to understand the purpose of them. The whole idea is to help you cope with indicating depth and distance by the use of cool and warm colour. They were done mainly as demonstrations in various countries such as Italy, Greece and America.

In the Venetian scene on the right, as always start from the back using pale cool colours. Notice the three distinctly different greens on the right. The stonework is done using various mixes of raw sienna, burnt umber and light red. I used the 1in flat, see pages 16-17. For example the bridge, boats and stonework are all done with it. You'll see I've left the area under the bridge as untouched paper to give the effect of dazzling light. As for the water, paint this in pale blue, and when this is dry add the reflected squiggles in similar colours to the objects behind them.

The main thing to look at in the painting below is the way that depth has been achieved by using very cool grey-greens in the distance, and rich reds and ochres in the foreground. Also, the direction of the brush strokes is very important here. The brush was used diagonally to show the slopes of the mountains, then vertically for the trees and the waterfall. Notice again how much use has been made of the white paper itself.

In the sunny scene on the right the distant shore is painted sparingly with absolutely no detail. The trees should be put in wet into wet before the sky is dry. Much use can be made of the white paper for highlights, but at the end, some of these may have to be covered up with a light wash to prevent the picture becoming too spotty. Restrict the true whites to the boats. Notice the strong warm colours on the beach, which are used to bring the picture forward. These are made from light red, raw sienna and burnt umber.

The main difficulty in this painting will be to keep the freshness and vitality. The water changes colour as it gets into the shadows and you can get this effect by adding a little raw sienna into the wet wash. While the sky, water and foreshore are painted with the hake, the 1in flat is used for the boats, hut and jetty.

The picture on the right was painted very fast, using a sort of graphic shorthand with staccato strokes of the 1in flat.

First paint the sky and distant hills, using them as negative shapes to show up the white house, which is untouched paper. The roofs are made from raw sienna and light red and the purple bougainvillea, is made from strong ultramarine and alizarin.

The shadows, which are very warm here, are light red and ultramarine. These should be put on very quickly and lightly to make them transparent, allowing the ground colour, very weak raw sienna, to show through. The same shadow mix is used on the left-hand building.

On this spread we have three tonal sketches for you to interpret in colour.

Starting from the back, after putting in the sky in the colour of your choice, put in the distant trees while the sky is still wet. Next paint the water, remembering that it must be the same colour as the sky. If you want sparkle, then do it in dry brush. The lighthouse, which is the main object of interest, can be rubbed out with a damp rag between two pieces of paper. Paint the top of the lighthouse carefully with touches of the 1in flat, dark against light.

Now move to the foreground rocks. These should be painted in warmer colours using burnt umber, raw sienna and a warm green. If you want help with the rocks, turn to page 78. The fishing boat just coming into harbour helps to balance the picture, and should be

very simply indicated with the 1in flat, as a silhouette against the light patch of sea.

The sketch below is of a village street in winter. The snow-laden sky should be graduated from top to bottom using a first wash of raw sienna, then a mixture of paynes grey with a touch of alizarin. If this is done

correctly, you'll get a realistic impression of an impending snow storm. Make the cottages fade into the distance, and warm the colours as you come forward. Leave white paper for the snow.

There are two ways of tackling this picture, depending on the sky you put in. You could make it cloudy and overcast, in which case your colours will be more subdued and you'd have no shadows, just patches of bare earth and rock.

Or you could make it a bright sunny day with a blue sky and patches of cloud, in which case you can use pale blue shadows from the trees to show the contours of the snow.

After putting in the sky, make the distant hillsides a mixture of ultramarine and light red, leaving bare paper for patches of snow.

The middle-distance trees should be painted with a mixture of burnt umber and raw sienna, not forgetting to counterchange some of the trunks while still damp, using your fingernail. Paint in the young saplings with the rigger and the main fir tree with the hake, in a rich olivey green.

The river you could put in with a darker tone of your sky colour. The shadows should be done very quickly, if you're putting them in, with a weak, pale ultramarine, adding the grasses with the rigger afterwards.

THE ELEMENTS

We have now covered the basics of watercolour and the handling of the paint with the different brushes - the thinness or thickness of the paint, and using the various strokes with a bit of confidence. We've got to turn now to techniques for indicating specific elements such as skies in all their moods; water in various forms whether it be a gentle brook, placid ponds, raging river torrents, or cold seas; trees and woods of all sorts whether near or far, in summer, autumn or winter dress; hills, even mountains, in all seasons; rocks and pebble beaches; buildings whether humble or grandiose; villages or cities and the people who inhabit them; flowers, those delicate and elusive things whose very fragility is so difficult to capture on paper.

All these elements present a challenge of their own, some easier than others, but you can succeed with patience and study. Clouds, for instance, seem impossible at first until you've learnt the right water content and gained confidence, but once mastered you can do half your painting in a couple of minutes with the hake. Figures need plenty of sketching to gain skill with them. To make convincing buildings you don't need to include every door, window or brick.

I try to do the minimum amount of work to get the maximum effect. Several of my painting heroes put less in and get more effect than I do. My ambition in a few years is to put half the strokes in and get twice as much money for the painting. You'll see how painting has similar characteristics to professional golf. Constantly endeavour to purify and simplify your painting but don't treat your audience like idiots. Let them do a lot of the work for themselves, and they'll always beat a path to your door.

This gentle river scene was painted in Scotland, and is a favourite type of subject. There is lots of wet into wet at the back with gradually strengthening tones as the scene moves towards the foreground. Painted entirely with the hake, rigger and the occasional fingernail, this was completed in about 20 minutes. Note that, as always, I've made good use of the white paper to give light and life to the scene.

57

Sky

In this section you're going to have to be prepared to waste some paper and persevere a bit! When I'm teaching, I usually leave this subject until the last day, by which time the students have got some confidence in their water/paint ratio.

Up until now they had probably produced skies which were timid and anaemic, choosing safety rather than taking the risk of spoiling the paper. These skies were usually plain blue or grey, merely forming a rather nondescript background to the scene. However, I'm hoping that by the time you get to the end of the section, you'll really enjoy the thrill and freedom of painting skies for their own sakes.

Your biggest ally will be your hake, with which you'll be able to cover the paper quickly. Timing is the most important thing. I find that the faster I paint them, the better they turn out. The biggest danger is the temptation to fiddle, and to touch them up afterwards while the paper is still wet. This should be strictly resisted!

Painting skies is mainly a question of confidence. The more you do, the easier they become. One of the problems is that most of us never look at the sky properly. You really do need to know a little about the different cloud formations before you can expect to paint them realistically, and the overall gauge of whether you've succeeded or failed, is if your sky is "believable" or not.

Although on page 62 you'll find a small 'do's and don'ts' section, I will point out some of the reasons for failure. After all it's only by avoiding these that you'll succeed. The two main villains are too much water, which produces runny clouds lacking in definition, and bad timing, by which I mean leaving too long between the various washes. This results in "cardboard cut-out" clouds. However, the satisfaction you'll get from producing a good sky will make all your hard work very worth while.

The thing to notice in this picture is that one large cloud dominates the whole sky. This should be used as a general rule in this type of sky painting. It's far better than putting two clouds of equal size side by side. Note too how the cloud balances the strong foreground bush. Try to get the sparkle on the water, relative to the blue sky above it, by using a dry brush.

CLOUD TYPES

The simplest sky of all is a perfectly blue one, but
even here you must use your skill to graduate it,
because the sky directly above you is always stronger
and richer than the horizon. Just go outside and take
a look!

Turning now to cloud formations we'll first look at
the cirrus clouds as in the picture on the right. Next
you should attempt the nimbus and the stratus
clouds. These are more threatening rain clouds.
Lastly, and far more difficult are the fluffy cumulus
clouds. Here you have to keep in mind several factors
before you start to paint. Firstly you don't actually
paint white clouds, you paint the blue sky around
them. Then, because of perspective, you will get a
huge cloud above you which would be at the top of
the page, and other clouds gradually diminish in size
as they recede towards the horizon. The next thing to
keep in mind is that a cumulus cloud is like a piece of
cotton wool held under a spot light, so that the top is
light while the underneath has a soft shadow.

For all the skies, I first put on a very pale cream
wash made from raw sienna with lots of water. I do
this very quickly and lightly, and once this is on, I
don't leave it to dry, but work quickly with my
succeeding washes so that the colours blend
together to some degree.

*Even with a perfectly blue sky, you still need to apply a wash
of very pale raw sienna with the hake, simply brushing
backwards and forwards until you reach the bottom. You must
immediately proceed to the next step while the wash is still
damp to get the right effect.*

*Now mix up some strong ultramarine, strong because it will
be weakened by the damp wash already on the paper. Work
backwards and forwards to establish a strongish blue at the
top, then proceed downwards gradually taking the pressure off
the brush until it's hardly touching the paper.*

Cirrus are very high clouds, which form streaks often called mares' tails. First apply your very weak raw sienna wash to the whole of the sky area, and while this is still damp, mix up some ultramarine, and with the hake make broad and light streaks right across the sky using the whole arm. It is the lightness and delicacy which gives you the character of the clouds. Never go back on them or you'll lose the quality. Don't forget that the blue must be lighter at the bottom of the sky.

Once you've finished the sky, sit back and watch it diffuse. Like all clouds, cirrus become smaller and narrower as they get to the horizon, and the highest one is always the one which is dominant. Also, remember that with clouds, you're painting in negative shapes – the cream forms the clouds.

To paint stratus start with a very weak wash of raw sienna, following the same procedure as in blue skies. Then mix up a strong mixture of paynes grey with a touch of alizarin, and make your first bold cloud at the top of the painting by working around the cloud shape.

Using this same wash, go backwards and forwards, making narrower and narrower clouds towards the horizon. It's very important that all this is done while the first wash is still damp. The slope of the paper and the action of diffusion will do the rest.

Never try to paint your skies with the paper completely flat. If the board is on a slope, you will find it easier to get the effects you need. In other words, you're using gravity as an aid. If you want a really rainy cloud, you can tip the board almost vertically.

The palette for these skies is restricted and all those on these pages can be done with raw sienna, ultramarine, paynes grey and alizarin crimson. As you gain confidence, you may want to bring in other colours, perhaps for dawn skies and sunsets, but do resist making them too gaudy. Finally, always think of your skies as an integral part of your landscape, setting the mood for the rest of the painting.

DO'S AND DONT'S

Do remember to make your clouds smaller the further away they are.

Do compensate for the water content in the first wash, by making the following wash stronger, using your rag to get rid of any excess water.

Don't try to push it around too much, let gravity do most of the work.

Don't use tissues to dab out clouds.

To produce basic cumulus clouds, paint round the clouds in blue onto the damp, weak raw sienna wash, making the clouds smaller as they recede to the horizon to capture the effect of perspective, and making the blue weaker as it goes into the distance.

Now comes the difficult bit, adding the paynes grey and alizarin to the undersides of the clouds, still before the raw sienna wash has dried, so that the paint diffuses. If it is too wet it will run away and if you leave it too long so that it's too dry, you'll be left with hard edges.

The cumulus sky above is produced by a weak wash of raw sienna, which shows through the sky, followed by ultramarine to pick out the cloud shapes. This is stronger at the top and weaker at the bottom. Now mix paynes grey with a touch af alizarin crimson to put in the undersides of the clouds.

Nimbus clouds (left) are more solid layered clouds. They're easier to do than cumulus as they have no light differential. The main problem is to get the right consistency and tones, so that they neither run away nor become too hard. The clouds on the left are in an evening sky, so I have added yellow to the first wash before painting in the clouds in paynes grey and alizarin.

On these two pages, we've come to more exciting weather conditions, which lend themselves better to watercolour than to any other medium. They're also perfect for the hake! Speed is even more essential with these skies, and the first raw sienna wash is the lubricant. Anything which goes on afterwards is given movement by it, always providing it is still wet. To avoid disappointment, these subsequent washes should be put on very strongly to compensate for the wet paper. They will inevitably diffuse and soften, but must still look strong when dry.

As with other cloud formations, they must be designed in your mind before you start, remembering again that one cloud should be allowed to dominate rather than having several of different size.

This painting (above) was great fun to do. If you want to reproduce this, you'll have to do the whole thing in just a couple of minutes. The timing on this could be a useful exercise in its own right. The sky is painted in three different layers. First the inevitable raw sienna wash, immediately followed by a stronger wash of raw sienna, paynes grey and alizarin. You'll see this as a medium tone. Now to the really strong stuff. Still working fast, put on a thick mixture of paynes grey and alizarin with great panache and courage, then stand back and watch it happen. You'll really enjoy the effects!

This (above right) is similar to the stormy sky, and the technique is much the same. Make the first raw sienna wash slightly wetter before you put on the paynes grey and alizarin mix, which should be quite strong to compensate. Then we come to the main difference which is to tip the picture almost vertically. The wash will then quickly diffuse downwards giving the effect of rain.

The secret of getting the effect for rain is to use a very wet initial wash and a steeply sloped board. You control the effect by the angle of your painting. So, as I said, we start with this very wet wash of raw sienna put on across the whole sky area, with the paper flat at this stage.

Now, immediately put on a strong secondary wash of paynes grey and alizarin and then tilt your painting quickly to get the right effect. Next, put in your hillside in strong paint, and if your timing is right, it will rain very realistically on the hillside.

Here we have more subtle, and therefore perhaps more difficult scenes. Their success is entirely dependent on timing and delicacy. Almost every student, right at the beginning, wants to know how to do sunsets, but in fact you need to learn all the other weather conditions first. Restraint is the keyword here.

Sunsets of course aren't just red. The top of the sky will often retain a delicate blue, running into yellow in the centre of the sky, and softest pinks on the horizon. Study them as much as you possibly can, preferably with your paints at the ready. Mists are my own favourite subject. They are almost a daily occurrence where I live and I have ample time to study them. The colours are very much greyed down, and there's a great chance to show off your wet-into-wet technique. Remember though, always to have something in your scene which is sharp and crisp to focus the eye, such as the foreground grasses in the picture opposite.

This very delicate, misty scene should be painted with a very limited palette. After the first wash of raw sienna, which should go down to the base of the hillside, apply a delicate mixture of paynes grey and alizarin across the top, allowing it to diffuse into the first wash. Now put on a stronger mixture for the hillside.

While this is still damp, add the middle-distance trees, with slightly stronger paint than for the hillside. For the river, paint over a wash to match the sky and add the reflections with downward strokes in stronger colour, sweeping out the shine with a dry brush. Finally, when everything is dry, paint in the foreground grasses. Notice how the white paper has been allowed to show through to add sparkle.

Start this tranquil sunset scene by putting on the usual raw sienna wash, but now add a delicate touch of blue across the top. In the middle add some yellow, and at the bottom a mixture of alizarin crimson and lemon yellow. This must all be done quickly! While this graduated wash is still wet, add your rich mixture of paynes grey and alizarin for the clouds. The variations on this simple routine are endless.

Practice

This is where you have to take your courage in both hands and go for it! On the next four pages I've shown you five different skyscapes. In each case the clouds are the main factor with only a small proportion of the painting taken up by the landscape. What I want you to do is to change the weather conditions.

For instance where I've shown you a clear blue sky, you could put in some cumulus clouds. Have a look back through this section to remind yourself of the various formations. Useful as this is, however, the best way is to go outside, or look out of your window and paint whichever kind of sky meets your eye. Some of our finest artists have done just that, practising until in time they could paint almost any weather conditions out of their heads. Many of the people I've taught have told me later that they find themselves looking at skies with new eyes. You can increase your knowledge by looking properly.

Don't try to be too ambitious at first. Keep to simple cloud shapes, and don't ever put too many in one painting, particularly all the same size. You can give your picture great depth by making a big difference between the front and back clouds.

This scene has a graduated blue sky and foreground interest. There's plenty of scope here to project your own personality. You might first try to put in wispy cirrus clouds, which would liven up the picture, but taking care of course to make them smaller near the horizon. You'll find some help on page 61. Alternatively, you could try some storm clouds, preferably coming in from the right to balance the landing stage. Finally, how about a sunset? Here you'll have to make a very subtle blend of blue, yellow and pink, before adding any clouds, with a mixture of paynes grey and alizarin. Don't forget, however, that you'll have to change the colour of the river to match the sky above. A big mistake could be to have a blue river beneath a stormy sky. (I've seen this happen often!).

The possibilities are endless. Try anything your imagination dictates – rain on the hillside, storm or sun. And remember all the points you've learned in the previous pages.

As you can see, the painting above is a cirrus sky, with one large dominant cloud. Try changing the mood of this completely by painting a really threatening stormy sky. First put on your pale raw sienna wash, then immediately mix up paynes grey with a small amount of alizarin. Now take a deep breath and make one large cloud right across the top of the picture. Below this add some diminishing parallel clouds in the same colour but leaving enough of the original raw sienna wash between them for the clouds to diffuse. You should find that this produces a very interesting effect. You can control the diffusion by the angle at which you hold the paper. The steeper the angle, the faster it will diffuse. To heighten the stormy effect, try putting some puddles in the road, preferably below the posts, so that they can be reflected.

Remember too that the colours below will be affected by the sky. They will be more sombre and there will be less sparkle.

The snow scene (top) can be handled in various ways. As it is, the yellow grey sky looks fairly benevolent. You could try a cloudless blue sky. The shadows from the trees would be blue, and you might put a pale cream wash over the snow to show the warmth of the sun. The distant hills would then be sharp and crisp. Then you could make the sky full of threatening snow by using the "rain" sky on page 65, in which case there would be hardly any shadows cast, except directly under the trees.

The very simple flat landscape above can also be handled in many ways. You'll notice the scene is in two distinct planes, the distant trees and the strong, rich foreground. The bush cries out for a very dark cloud on the top left to balance it, so make it a stormy sky as on page 65. If you make it a cumulus sky, you should make the distant trees sharper, put some shadows beneath the clouds, and brighten up your greens.

This looks a more elaborate and ambitious landscape, but it is still straightforward. The thing to remember is to change the colour of the river to match the sky. If you want, for instance, to make it a sunset, the river might be a mixture of pink and yellow, but any clouds should be on the right to help balance the large tree. You'll find help for this on page 68.

Now how about making this a misty scene using the techniques shown on page 67? The colours of course would be much more subdued, and the distant trees merely a whisper. The sky would graduate from grey to cream, and the river would match it. Only the foreground bank would be at full strength to exaggerate the recession. Finally, you could make it into a snow scene with bare winter trees and a cirrus sky, in which case the shadows on the far bank and under the trees would be blue. You'll find help with this on page 61.

Water

Water is one of the subjects that lends itself ideally to watercolour. Once you've learned the basic ways of portraying it you'll find yourself looking for "watery" subjects. The results can be very rewarding. What you've really got to learn is to represent water in its various forms and I'm going to show you here how to do it. Think of three different types of water. Firstly, motionless, as in a pond, a puddle or a placid river. Secondly, ruffled as in an exposed lake or a harbour. And finally, rushing and rough, as in a fast-moving rocky river or the sea. Each has its own character and needs to be treated in a different way.

MOTIONLESS WATER

First, it's not as it's often painted by beginners, universally blue with little squiggles to represent ripples. Water itself, although having no colour, reflects everything around it. The colour of the sky, be it blue, cloudy, grey or the golden yellow of a sunset, will cause the water to change colour too.

I first painted the distant forest (right) wet-into-wet with stronger, thicker colour on the left, the top part of the river, being relatively unruffled, reflects what is behind it. The rushy water in front I painted with fast, light strokes of the hake in the direction of the flow, giving a dry brush effect and leaving plenty of untouched paper to look like foam. The rock on the right is also painted quickly and economically with lots of rich paint.

In the illustration below with its calm stretch of water and foreground puddle, I did the sky and sea in one go. I first put a wash of yellow and raw sienna over the white paper, then added a streak of alizarin crimson across the middle and some clouds with paynes grey and alizarin crimson.

When it was dry I held a piece of paper on the horizon and wiped off a streak with a sponge to represent the shine on the sea. I then mixed up some strong foreground colour and painted it in quickly leaving the puddle showing through. It does show graphically the colour reflections.

Water itself has no colour whatsoever, but when it's still and motionless, it reflects everything around it. The colour of the sky above whether it is blue, cloudy, or the rich, golden yellow sunset, makes the water appear to change colour. As you look at still water, the rocks, the banks and trees behind will appear in it just like a mirror. But along comes a breeze ruffling the water, and immediately the reflections soften and break up. This usually happens on a large stretch of water with a fair amount of wind around. You don't see the reflection of distant objects, but close-up objects will still reflect.

Now let's look at some of the things that go wrong. A common mistake is to paint lots of fussy ripples. This will create the wrong effect. Another common fault is to draw and paint rivers that go uphill and tip up as they go round bends. This is always due to not looking enough at the river itself before it is drawn.

A winter scene on the river using mainly the hake. This is achieved by starting with a quick wash for the sky in pale blue. While the wash is still wet, the distant trees can be added, varying the colour with burnt umber and blue, and a touch in places of raw sienna. To add the main tree (which is the focal point of the picture) paint of the same colours can be used.

The river is now added with fairly wet blue (not straight from the tube, but subtly toned down). While the paint is still wet, a strong mixture of burnt umber and ultramarine dropped on to the wash below the tree will create a reflection. The posts were put in with a touch of the 1in flat and the reflections of the bushes were created with the same mixture.

To complete the picture the hake should first be put into the waterpot and then dried to make it "thirsty". If this is immediately drawn across the big dark tree reflection before the paint has dried, this will take off the paint and leave a streak to show where a slight breeze ruffles the water. The streak should always be horizontal.

The hills in the painting on the left were created with one stroke of the 1in flat using a mixture of light red and ultramarine. While that was still damp, a mixture of raw sienna and light red was added. This was much thicker paint so that it didn't run away. The effect of the shoreline is created by leaving some white paper to sparkle.

For the reflections, a light, thin wash of ultramarine was used while still damp, and the light red and ultramarine mountains were dropped in. Some thick tree colour was then touched in on top of the mountain reflections. The trunks were put in with the fingernail while the paint was still damp.

In this painting a slight breeze has ruffled the water so there are no reflections from the far shore. This was painted with mixtures of burnt umber and ultramarine. For the water a subtle blue can be mixed followed by one quick, very light sweep with the hake to try and get sparkle on the water. Finally, the foreground reeds are added with the rigger and the post with the 1in flat. These reflect but are "wobbly" and have no detail. The shore should be done very quickly with a warm mixture of burnt umber and raw sienna.

RUFFLED WATER

When a breeze comes along and breaks up the surface distant objects don't reflect at all, but close objects do in a "wiggly" way. You can create these reflections with vertical, wiggly brush strokes or light, directional strokes. Use the white of the paper to create the light catching the tops of ripples.

The picture below was painted in Tennessee. The water at the back reflects some of the colour behind it but not any objects. When it gets to the foreground it hits the rocks and breaks up into foam. This is very exciting to paint, especially with the hake. I use very fast, light directional strokes, leaving lots of white paper.

The background trees have been painted wet into wet using pale ultramarine and a little yellow, and then adding dark rich green made from paynes grey and yellow on the left to bring it forward. Vertical strokes have been used here.

Horizontal strokes of the same colour were used to create the background river. For the big vertical rock on the right I used a mixture of burnt umber, blue and raw sienna, painted richly and quickly.

RUSHING AND ROUGH WATER

This is when the water is shown as a fast-moving river over rocks or as a very rough sea showing strong waves. Use quick, directional brush strokes to create a sense of movement in the water, and leave patches of white paper for the crests of waves.

In the scene on the left there are three layers of distance. The far hillside is painted in pale ultramarine, the forward hillside is warmer through the addition of light red to the mixture. Directional strokes have been used to show the slope, changing to green on the flat. From the wall forward strong rich warm colour with browns and reds have been used. The last thing to paint is the river, using sky colour and leaving parallel rows of white paper untouched.

Below is really a close-up of a waterfall. Notice how much white paper is left untouched. This is contrasted with the surface of the water behind which is a dark rich colour made from ultramarine and burnt umber. At the bottom of the falls, move forward using calligraphy to indicate the swirling water. You can also use the corner of a Stanley knife blade to convey spray and sparkle when the paint is dry.

ROCKS

"I can't paint rocks." I've heard that said so many times from anguished students, as if there was something mysterious and baffling about them. They usually turn out "cardboard cutouts" with very little, or no, shape about them.

Look at the rocks in the painting on the opposite page. The top faces the light, so it has lighter tone than the sides. I created its surface with a quick light stroke of the hake to show its texture. I painted the sides darker, using downward strokes, and it immediately looked solid and heavy. As to the colours of rocks, use anything except green, which is the colour of grass, and can be confusing. I use varying amounts of brown and blue together, but do vary the colours. In sunshine, paint some warm bright colours at the base to show light bouncing off the ground into the shadows.

Try not to be boring and make all your rocks the same size, shape and colour. If you're painting a ground, vary the distance between them, and always put larger rocks in the foreground, and smaller in the distance to give the illusion of depth.

Think of a rock as a hard, heavy thing. Just spend a few minutes looking at the rocks on these pages and you'll realize how much the direction of the brush stroke helps. Notice, too, how I've put some contrasting free brush strokes round the base.

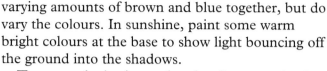

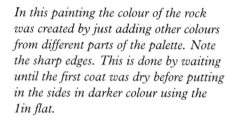

In this painting the colour of the rock was created by just adding other colours from different parts of the palette. Note the sharp edges. This is done by waiting until the first coat was dry before putting in the sides in darker colour using the 1in flat.

Here the side of a credit card was used to scrape away the paint from the top of the rock after painting the whole shape first. This creates dimension. By flicking with the little fingernail while the paint is still damp, you can indicate grass.

For a more rounded rock, the sides were added before the first wash was really dry. The warm colour of the ground "bounces back" into the shadow. Notice the quick light strokes on the ground, which gives texture to the whole painting.

On the opposite page, the rocks are given strength by rapid directional strokes. The hake is ideal for the tops, but the 1in flat can sometimes be used for the sides.

SEA

Sea can be very exciting to paint in watercolour once you've realized watercolour's limitations. You can only symbolize the wave forms and spray, but by using the white paper and fast brush strokes you can capture the atmosphere and movement of the water.

The colours and patterns on the sea are constantly changing, and it is worth spending a few minutes studying them before you begin. Then try to get down an impression of the colours and light, making brush strokes in the direction of movement of the water.

The colour of the sea is influenced by the sky, and it is not one flat colour. Work subtle variations of colour into it, and alternate light and dark patches to add to the sense of movement on the surface, letting small patches of paper show through for crests of waves and light reflecting on the water.

Watercolours allow for a quick, spontaneous treatment letting accidental effects add to the overall result, and this can be very effective in the sea. You might want to try putting on washes of different colours over the sea area and let them mix.

The rows of waves were coming forward in parallel rows, gradually receding into the distance. There I used very fast light strokes of the hake to get sparkle and movement, and change the colour of the sea, bluer at the back and greener at the front – never make it a boring all-over blue – it just isn't like that in reality. Notice how I've added the edge of the cliff to the bottom left-hand corner, partly to give another dimension but also to emphasize the high wind with the bent-over grasses, using quick directional strokes with the hake and rigger.

This is a very calm estuary scene that shows a few middle distance reflections of colour, but not on the far horizon. It's the foreground beach that is most interesting here. With the hake I've made broad, free sweeping strokes, basically raw sienna and burnt umber, leaving a few areas for puddles. Do this very quickly to keep it fresh.

The rocks in front were done in two stages, first an all-over pale wash and when this was dry darker, richer directional strokes with the hake for the sides of the rocks.

This breaking wave painting is a combination of hard and soft edges. Paint the sky first, then the distant cliff and sea in soft tones leaving the wave as white paper.

The rocks are painted in hard, in browns and light red and softened off afterwards with a hog's hair brush. Ultramarine and lemon yellow were mixed to make the foreground sea with the dark holes and calligraphy added afterwards.

Lastly dampen the wave itself with clear water and drop in a touch of blue wet into wet here and there.

The painting below shows the technique of painting close-up boats and reflections on disturbed water. Students are often afraid to use dark, rich colours on water, but sometimes they're needed, as you can see in this picture. There were strong contrasts above so they had to show in the water.

I left the water until last and looked at it for a few minutes before I painted it to get the general feel of it – this is very important. Then I painted it with the sky colour, avoiding the boat reflections. While the wash was still wet I painted in the darks with a mixture of burnt umber and blue. Finally, when everything was dry I added a bit of calligraphy on top. The ropes and stays I did with quick strokes of a Stanley knife blade afterwards.

The painting on the right is mainly about the foreground shore, which seems to cause such difficulty for students. What I try to do is to paint my first coat of colour as fast and light as possible, which allows some sparkle to show through, at the same time addding other colours to give some variety.

When this is dry I add some stronger colour and texture over just part of the beach, leaving much of the original wash showing through. To get more texture I often use my knuckle in the still damp paint. The rocks on this painting were done with a credit card. Generally I feel the speed of application is very important – a quick stroke always looks more exciting and spontaneous than a slow one.

Practice

You will notice on these pages three paintings with scenes surrounding water. The water areas have been left blank.

Copy the scenes one by one. By using the knowledge you've hopefully gained so far and referring to this chapter, it is now time for you to complete the pictures. Don't hesitate to look again at previous pages. For example, the lower painting on page 74 will be useful when you're working on the first exercise. You'll notice the strokes for the reflections are dropped in virtually from the shore-line. Remember that the darker you want the reflections, the thicker the paint should be.

In this scene the bottom has been left blank for you to fill in. Imagine the water as still. First paint the water roughly the colour of the sky, then drop in the reflections of the various hills and trees into the water while the first wash is still damp. Make sure the reflections are a soft upside-down mirror image of the objects behind, with the colours and tone roughly the same.

In this picture, imagine the water as smooth with mirror images. Then paint the same picture with a fast-flowing river with no reflections, but with lots of movement in the river. It's going round an S-bend so your brush strokes should show this. Don't forget to leave plenty of white paper to indicate foam.

Copy this woodland scene, but then add a really fast-flowing stream with rocks. Make the directions of the brush indicate the speed and direction of the water. Paint the rocks in mid-stream larger at the front and smaller at the back. If you need some help, look at the way I've treated the water in the top picture on page 76.

This is a tonal sketch painted in burnt umber. Now turn it into a full colour painting. Try using autumn colours, and then some summer greens. For autumn I suggest the distance is in mauve made out of ultramarine and light red and put on thinly, then come forward using burnt umber, raw sienna and light red. For summer use yellow, ultramarine, paynes grey and raw sienna. The painting on page 79 will help you.

On the left is a very wet-into-wet sky just painted round the main wave, the edge of which should be partly hard and partly soft. I cheat a bit here by using a small hog's hair oil-painting brush and clean water to soften the edges where necessary. The distant sea can be painted very quickly leaving white paper in places. A mixture of ultramarine and lemon yellow can be used for the foreground. This should be very wet, with wild quick strokes to keep it flowing and fresh.

Finally little holes were added in dark green and a few squiggles were put in with the rigger to indicate rivulets. You can never hope to represent the sea precisely. You can create effective impressions by showing, foam, spray, holes and rivulets. These should be painted as freshly and quickly as possible. The main thing is not to overwork it and avoid fiddling afterwards.

On the opposite page is a typical estuary scene. The fluffy cumulus clouds suggest that there is probably a breeze blowing. You wouldn't therefore get any reflections from the distant shore, but the nearby post would reflect in the puddle. I've tried to indicate some buildings on the far shore – just a hint really. With the foreground beach interesting texture needs to be shown without making it muddy: a few bits of grass with the rigger, a rock or two using a credit card and some variation in colour. Notice how the birds, which link the three areas of the painting, are counterchanged light against dark, dark against light.

This is a calm seascape with the main emphasis on the rocky foreshore. I've tried to keep it fresh and vigorous by using broad strong sweeps with the hake to indicate fairly flat, smooth rocks. Notice that you can avoid monotonous colour by introducing blue and raw sienna into the brown. If raw sienna is

added as it comes nearer the shore it will show the colour of the sand beneath.

The yacht can be added by using two pieces of paper for a mask and a damp rag. Take two pieces of thin card and overlap them to form an inverted 'V'. Then using a dampened rag I rub the paint off.

Trees

I've found that the hake is a tremendous help when painting trees. It prevents you totally from attempting to put every leaf on the tree – always a terrible temptation – and forces you to see trees as masses, whether you're looking at a single tree or at woodland. After all we're not botanists, and our job as artists is to convey the mood of the scene, whether it's an early morning walk in the woods, or the joyous glow of an autumn woodland. We're trying to create a symbol of a tree that is instantly recognizable by the viewer.

You'll find in this chapter trees in all their forms, both singly and en masse. Speaking of "en masse", one of the most difficult things is to prevent artists from portraying a wood as a collection of individual trees. When trees are growing in a group, they lose their own identity and become part of the mass. As you look through this chapter, you'll soon see the truth of this statement. Another common fault is to paint receding trees, either woodland or in an open landscape, all the same green. You'll find aerial perspective plays a very large part when you're depicting trees. I always try to exaggerate and exploit this factor when I'm painting landscapes.

DO'S AND DONT'S

Do leave gaps in the foliage and only show the branches in the gaps.

Do paint the foliage with the lightest of touches with the hake.

Do learn to control the rigger with confidence. It can be a true friend!

Don't paint in 6m (20ft) high twigs, learn to taper from trunk to branches to twigs.

Don't paint cardboard cutout trees. They always have soft edges with lots of skyholes.

Let's look now at the practical side, and learn some basic facts about painting trees. A tree tapers gradually upwards from its own trunk, right to the tiny twigs at the end of the branches. The skill is in using brush control to show this very gradual diminishing. Always start at the base of the tree and work up, after all that's the way it grows! You'll find lots of exercises in the following pages which will help you to overcome the basic faults.

The basic tree should be done first with the hake, lightly indicating the foliage and leaving plenty of skyholes. Then the branches are added with the rigger, showing them only where the gaps in the foliage occur, and tapering them to the extremities of the tree. It's really worth practising this over and over again.

Opposite we have a gentle walk through a tree-lined avenue in summer. The feeling of depth is achieved by using cool blue greens at the back, with no detail, and using rich, strong contrasting greens at the front. The dappled light on the avenue is created by using alternating stripes of light red and ultramarine put in quickly.

The scene is given a focal point by the introduction of the two figures. They also lend scale. When painting the light and dark greens on the right of the picture, put in the light greens first. Let them dry, then put in the dark greens, allowing the light wash to show through occasionally.

On the left you'll find a page from my sketchbook showing various trees in different seasons of the year. Notice how few strokes I've used. In the winter trees I've used my dry-brush hake to show the twigs. I've tried to get plenty of colour into the big trunk. Don't think of it as all-over brown, they never are, there are always lots of subtle colours there.

With the two distant scenes at the bottom of the page, I've tried to give an impression of lots of things going on in a simple way, by using directional strokes. These take only seconds to do, but are very effective. They rely very much on using contrasting tone values.

My trunks are almost always constructed from sideways strokes of the hake, rather than an upwards sweep, as it seems to give them more character. I then use my rigger to depict the branches and twigs. The two important things here, are to remember to make the branches quite substantial as they leave the trunk, and to diminish them in size as they move outwards.

Another thing to remember is to step your branches. Do not to have them coming off opposite each other. Finally, if you make the branches cross over each other, you'll create more depth.

The painting above, of autumn trees, shows how the various species can be indicated in a very simple way. They merely give an impression without detail. An important point to note here is the way the general colours are affected in the water, painted wet into wet over the blue. You'll see too that the far distant trees are just hinted at in a simple mass.

When you try doing this picture give yourself a time limit – I did this in about 4 minutes. This way you'll retain the freshness. You'll notice again the limited palette of burnt umber, raw sienna and paynes grey.

In this scene, the season has been changed by using summer colours and altering the matching reflections in the water. Start from the back using very cool blue green, fairly weak, and mix the colours more strongly and with more yellow for the nearer group of trees.

Try to vary the texture and colour as much as possible, using the rigger and your fingernail to depict the trunks and branches. Don't forget the shine on the water produced by a quick sweep of a thirsty hake while the reflections are still damp.

In these two pictures I've tried to show you the tiny amount of detail required when depicting woodland scenes at various distances, while still retaining the credibility of the scene.

The one above shows some vague indication of separate trees in the front, but quickly resolves into an all-over mass behind. Note too the limited use of the rigger to show bare trees, and the dry-brush hake on the right.

In the picture on the right the woods are even further away, and so there is correspondingly less explanation. These trees are almost entirely portrayed by the profile at the top.

This woodland scene is depicted in three different seasons of the year, summer, autumn and winter.

In the autumnal scene on the previous page, I've used raw sienna, burnt umber and light red to produce the glowing colours of autumn.

In the winter scene, above, greys and browns are predominant, and the scene has been simplified even more. Although basically cold, there are touches of ochre and russet giving warmth to various parts of the picture, to avoid all-over bleakness. There's also a pale tone of raw sienna over the snow and I've added the shadows to give a feeling of misty sunshine.

The colours used to convey the feeling of the warmth of summer, opposite, are lemon yellow, paynes grey, ultramarine and raw sienna with the addition of light red for the path and shadows.

These doodles show how the hake and
the rigger can produce impressions of
foreground texture quickly and
spontaneously. Try to avoid the danger
of over-working these, as they can get
muddy very quickly. Use the rigger and
your fingernail to depict the grasses and
a credit card for the tops of the rocks.

Practice

Here are some exercises for painting trees and incorporating them into different scenes. On this page are some groups of trees to copy. Remember to treat them "en masse" rather than as individual trees. Then try adding some groups of trees to the open landscape, thinking carefully about where you position them. The woodland scene needs finishing off. With individual trees, practise using the rigger to control the gradual tapering of the branches by varying the pressure on the brush.

These are two groups of trees. As a guide you can do them in about a couple of minutes when you've had a bit of practice. You can use the corner of the hake very lightly with different strengths of paint, weak at the back and stronger at the front. If you do a page of trees you will learn an enormous amount about handling your brushes, especially by trying the winter trees with the rigger. The twigs at the top are shown by very gentle and delicate touches with the corner of the hake.

This landscape with clouds and distant hills looks a bit bleak and empty – it's meant to! It's there for you to add distant woods and nearer groups of trees in front of them. The distant woods, wherever you put them, should be mere tones relying on their top profile to suggest that they're trees, and keeping their colours cool and restrained.

With the nearest groups of trees, you can afford to be bolder, adding more detail, warmer colours and contrast. Mind you don't make one side or the other of the picture top heavy. However, a distant wood on one side might balance a nearby group very nicely. Avoid the mistake of putting the top of a tree touching the sky line. It should be either above or below it.

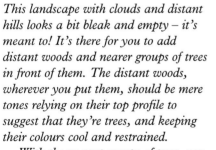

This woodland scene also looks a little sparse. I've just provided it to give you a start. I'd like to re-paint the scene giving it more depth, cooling the background by using more ultramarine in the mixture. Use the rigger to draw the distant trees into the still damp wash. Then gradually make the greens richer and warmer as you work forward. By this time the original wash will have begun to dry off, and your more forward trees will be sharper. Now to the main foreground tree on the left. Add more branches and leaves, generally make it the most important tree in the painting.

Finish the painting by putting in the ground texture and undergrowth. This could be fairly plain at the back but becomes more specific as you come towards the front of the scene. Look at some of the textures in the paintings on pages 96 and 97, particularly those in the bottom right-hand corner.

You might even try a little path through the woods, but make it curve the opposite way from that on page 96.

Here we have a woodland stream on a misty summer morning. I want you to change the seasons – see pages 95-7.

So let's start with autumn. After drawing very roughly the shape of the stream (don't make it go uphill), put the sky in by painting a very pale raw sienna wash. This should extend to the bottom of the distant trees, then just darken the top of the sky with ultramarine. Then make up some medium-strength mauve out of ultramarine and bright red, and paint the distant trees right across the background. Whilst the first raw sienna wash is still damp, add an occasional strip of pure raw sienna.

Next, build up the trees as they move forward, using a mixture of raw sienna and light red with occasional use of burnt umber. This is mostly wet into wet. Thicken the paint as you work towards the front. Notice the occasional strokes of the hake on the ground. The colour of the reflections in the stream should match the trees, but is still dropped in wet into wet on a pale blue surface.

Before you attempt a winter version of this with snow on the ground, study the painting on page 96. Here the palette is much more restrained using mainly greys and browns, and a few warm reds and tans.

As we come to close-up woodland scenes, we have further problems getting the feeling of depth. This I try to do by painting the back wet into wet with cool colours, using the rigger to put in distant trunks. Then come the sharper richer colours at the side of the painting. As the first overall wash dries, the trees become sharper and more defined, and I alternate between the rigger and hake to get the effects. By the time I reach the front of the painting everything is dry, and the branches and foreground grasses are sharper. The dappled shadows should be done very quickly and lightly allow the underneath colours to show.

Buildings and Street Scenes

I was recently teaching in the beautiful city of Venice. Four architects were on the course, and for the first few days, at the evening sessions, these beautifully drawn scenes would turn up. Paintings of rich old buildings by canals with every window carefully counted and indicated, complete with the correct number of frames – perfect, but so sterile, they looked like modern office blocks! It took me a few days to make them realize that suggestion was so much more fun, especially in a city like Venice. Their buildings began to look weathered and mellow, and varied in colour.

Most painters take very easily to the idea that they can symbolize hills, trees, fields and rivers, but when it comes to buildings they seem to freeze up. All their early confidence goes, and they become tight and rigid. The main reason seems to be that

The quick sketch on the left captures the atmosphere of Venice. You need make no attempt to put in every window, but try to leave a few whites such as the balcony and the lines of the bridge, and vary the colours of the walls as much as possible.

On the right is a straightforward street scene. You might try having a go at it yourself. The main difficulty is getting the perspective, but there should be no problems if you follow the principles on page 105. Once it's drawn in roughly, put the sky in with the hake with a graduated wash of ultramarine on top of neat raw sienna.

Then, before you even think of any details, paint the walls and road in varying colours. Don't stick to one boring colour for each wall, but add other colours from your palette as you work. Don't put in the dark shadow yet.

When the first washes are dry, change over to the 1in flat, and put in most of the windows, doors and awnings, keeping the brushwork free and fast. Then with the rigger, indicate the figures, and put in the dark shadow on the wall.

terrible word "perspective", which strikes fear into many earnest would-be painters. You can, once you've got over the fear, learn enough about perspective in an hour to keep you out of trouble for ever afterwards. In actual fact once you've got your basic drawing right, your audience will accept a building without much detail. Conversely, if your drawing is wrong from the start, no matter how much detail and brickwork you put in afterwards you will not succeed in making it look right and

convincing. So keep your buildings very simple.

It's this word "convincing" that's so important. A distant town on a hillside can look convincing with a few roofs, windows and trees (look at that on page 104). It's not laziness on my part. Anything more than that and it will look tired and overworked, and certainly no more true to life. The problem is to convince my art students of this, as they patiently draw in every detail.

I'm sorry to be so negative, but the next thing

In this scene the distant group of buildings has been painted with the minimum of brush strokes. The buildings themselves have been treated as simple abstract shapes. The paper has been left white for most of the walls, with a hint of shadow on some side walls. The roofs have been put in with single brush strokes as quite rough shapes, and quick flicks with the edge of the brush have been used for the windows.

that shows up over and over again is an all-over flatness and lack of punch for so much work. This is mainly due to two things and is fortunately easily curable. One is lack of counterchange between a building and whatever is behind it, be it a tree, a hillside or even another building. It's no good putting a red roof against a green tree, both in the same tone, relying on the differences in colour to separate the two things – it doesn't work. Either lighten the roof or darken the tree. I'm often told

indignantly, "Well it was the same tone!" That's no excuse. One of your jobs as an artist is to make your picture "read easily", so often you have to exaggerate to differentiate things on paper – in other words to "cheat a bit".

The other main fault is to paint the adjacent side of a building the same tone, relying on a line of what I call "wire" to show where the corner comes. Always decide on where your light is coming from, and make the side facing the light much lighter in

Here are a couple of those building drawings that amateur painters skip over quickly to get to the more interesting bits of the book, and then complain that they know nothing about perspective. Please just spare ten minutes to look at them both.

You'll see that if you draw in the base of the building and the roof line, and project them, the line will meet at an imaginary point called the focal point. Draw lines back from this and you've got all the angles for the windows and doors straight away. It's easy! and it's the main principle of perspective.

To get the angles right for your first two lines along the gutter and base, just hold out your pencil at arms length, lay it over the lines concerned and judge the angle it makes in relation to the horizontal. You'll soon learn to get it right every time, and very quickly too.

tone than the side facing away. It sounds so logical and common sense doesn't it? But this is often ignored. It's sometimes a good idea to put a pencil cross at the top right or left corner to remind you of the light source.

Now let's talk about shadows; these are an enormous help to the artist in describing form, but particularly when it comes to buildings. On one of

my videos is a demonstration of a street scene with shops. I show it on my painting courses and there's always an audible gasp as I put the main shadow in at the end – it makes such a dramatic difference to the painting.

There are two sorts of shadows; one, the form shadow, we've already talked about, which makes the side away from the light source darker and

Shadows in street scenes are enormously important. To show this, I've done two little paintings of a town square in France, firstly on the left without any shadows, giving a very flat and uninspired look. It might as well be a cardboard cutout of the scene, because it has no depth.

In the version on the left the shadows under the roofs, balcony and awning show the overhang of each. The shadow between the two facing buildings thrusts the right one out by counterchange and completely separates them. Even the shadows at the base of the figures hold them on the ground and give them substance.

appears to give form and substance to the building. There is also the cast shadow, which is caused by something interrupting the light, like a gutter, which casts a shadow below it, and shows the viewer in an instant that it is protruding over the wall below. So when you combine the form and cast shadows, they describe buildings so easily to the viewer that fiddly details become unnecessary, and you can get away with making very few strokes to create solidity.

Always try to avoid muddy opaque shadows. They should be transparent enough to allow the underneath wall colour to show through. I always use a thinnish mixture of light red and ultramarine, which I add at the end of my painting.

This is why a master painter like Edward Seago's simple economical buildings look so satisfying and

These two illustrations are all about counterchanging. A dark tree put in behind the corner of a light roof will dramatize the roof.

On the left, the trees highlight the barn, but the rear end of the barn being dark is counterchanged against the light sky, and the objects in front are left light too.

The buildings in the picture below are full of counterchange. The top of the wall on the left is light against the dark house, and the front facing wall is dark against the cottages behind.

The dark figures against the light wall help too. If they had been coming down the steps, they would have had to be light.

descriptive, whilst so many amateur over-worked and fussy buildings seem to look flat and boring.

I find that using the 1in flat almost exclusively for my buildings prevents me from over-working the details, which can just be suggested.

Another problem people create for themselves when they're doing a street scene is that they try to draw each house individually and then join them together. This is like trying to paint a wood by painting each separate tree. This is true particularly in places like Venice. It's far better to use one overall wash that will cover the whole street, dropping in other colours to give variety. When this is dry, add windows, doors etc., again in a loose way, using the corner of the 1in flat for the windows, and touching the flat side of the brush to the paper for such things as gutters and balconies.

Let's look at the colours in buildings. You have probably seen many paintings of walls in one flat dull colour with no variety. The way to get exciting-

These are all architectural details made with the 1in flat, painted lightly and with the minimum pressure on the brush.

Railings, gates and medium-distance roof tiles are made by touching the paper with the edge of the brush. Try copying these examples

very quickly using the minimum of strokes with fairly dry paint, too much water and you'll lose all the texture.

By learning to angle the brush in different directions, you'll soon be able to indicate anything from a balcony to a portico.

Here are a few features you can include on roofs and walls. It is important to vary the colours on walls. Once the first layer has dried, add one or two colours to indicate natural stonework or brickwork. Once the viewer sees this, they assume the rest of the surface is the same. It just becomes tedious to put in every brick. The same applies to planks on doors and sheds.

In the simple barn on the right, note how these textures can be applied to a building. Look how the roof has been graduated. It is dark on the left against the sky and lighter on the right.

looking buildings is to add different colours, a bit of blue, or raw sienna or light red to the basic wash. This will give a far more vital and glowing appearance. Once this colourful wash is dry, a few judicious hints of stone or brickwork using the 1in flat will be sufficient.

The variation of colour applies not only to the walls and houses, but also to the surface of the streets themselves. People seem to have great difficulty in finding the right colour for the road surface, and often finish up with an overall dull grey, which kills the painting stone dead! Try therefore to apply the same principals to the roads as you do to the walls. If the street is a cobbled one just indicate a few cobbles in the immediate foreground rather than through the whole area.

Don't be put off by my list of pitfalls. Street scenes can be very exciting and great fun to do. Remember, the less work you put into them, the better they will be!

Here are three vignettes of buildings – a boat-house, barns and a church – all done mostly with the 1in flat brush, only using the hake to indicate the ground and the trees. Even with the trees, it is best to change brushes half way through to get the sharp edges round the buildings. The masts and gate should be done by just touching the edge of the 1in flat quickly on the paper.

Opposite is a typical street scene. Though it's a higgledy piggledy collection of shops of various heights and ages, all follow the same basic perspective. Just draw the pavement line and the general roof line and make them meet. The various window angles can be drawn from this focal point. Vary the colours of the walls as much as possible to avoid monotony, and paint them in first, together with the street, before you start any doors and windows. Awnings and signs can be used to add bright colours. Note the figures. Although they are different heights, the heads are more or less on the same level.

Practice

On these two pages, I'm setting tasks for you to tackle for yourselves – adding shadows, putting in windows and doors, and creating your own houses and a village in an existing landscape. In each of the four projects you'll find lots of different ways to complete the paintings, and you could try more than one alternative for each.

In most of the work, you'll mainly need the 1in flat, using it in various ways to create a roof, or a window or door. It is a good idea to use a piece of tracing paper on each picture to do most of your initial drawing, and then transfer it to your watercolour paper – too much rubbing out and alterations spoil the surface of the paper.

Here I've left the profile of the village for you to fill in just by indicating roofs, shadows and windows. Of course you don't have to use my profile, you could make your own adding a church or a tree in the middle of the village. Put your houses at different angles. With regard to shadows, try making the light source come first from one side, and then the other. Also put a few people in your village. Don't make all the roofs the same colour, vary them from pink to grey.

Here's a completely deserted hillside and field. All it needs is perhaps a white cottage counterchanged against the trees, or perhaps a little village further up on the hillside. Try to remember about counterchange all the time. It could be a village on the skyline, dark against the sky, or fairly light against the darkish hillside. It would probably need a little lane going to it, perhaps starting wide at the bottom right corner, winding through the picture and tapering into the distance.

Here's a more desirable residence that needs shadows added to it to complete it. Try it two ways, one with the light coming from the left, in which case the right hand wall would be in shadow, and the end wall lit up, and don't forget the shadows from the chimneys and dormer windows too. If you add a figure or two, the direction of their shadows would vary.

On the left is a group of buildings, or a farm that's been extended over the years. It's for you to decide where to put the windows and doors in, and perhaps porches. You might decide on a French theme and add coloured shutters to the windows. Use the corner of the 1in flat by tipping the brush over. Don't expect to get nice, perfectly square windows (see the illustration above). You can also use the edge of the brush to get windowsills and doorframes etc.

People and Animals

Many people feel nervous about adding figures and animals into their paintings. They think it's going to ruin their painting right at the end, after they've spent a long time working on it – far better to leave it empty!

It is true that a bad figure can spoil a landscape, but with a little preparation and forethought, figures can greatly enhance a painting, providing human scale and making a main object of interest for the whole design.

If you look at the figures and animals on these two pages, you'll see how simple and lacking in detail they are. It is just a matter of getting the proportions and the attitude right. The main faults are always the same – painting the heads too big and making everyone stand to attention. Position people so that they are standing over things, or put their hands in their pockets. If a couple are standing or walking together, join them into one unified shape and don't try to put in any detail.

This applies too, if you have a crowd. People lose their individual shapes and identities and blend into a crowd shape. If you're still scared, work out your figures on another piece of paper until you're satisfied with them, then transfer them to your main painting by tracing them off. That will also help you to get the size and position right – another fear of the beginner.

DO'S AND DONT'S

Do make your figures fit in as part of the picture – not stuck on as appendages.

Do counterchange your figures – a light one against a dark background.

Do remember to put shadows from your figures – it anchors them to the ground.

Do try to make your figures tall, slim and elegant rather than stumpy dwarfs.

Don't make your figures too detailed.

Don't make their heads too big – that's the biggest fault with beginners.

Don't forget to join figures together as one unit to make a pair or a crowd.

The animals and birds above are not intended to be paintings on their own but included in a landscape. They should possess no detail – they could be almost silhouettes as long as they are indicated with delicacy. Try adding them to your own finished paintings. Although they must be drawn carefully beforehand, they should be painted in quickly to match the rest of the painting.

The various figures on the left, too, are done very quickly – and notice none of them have any feet! Feet seem to be unnecessary in landscape figures, indeed they always seem to look clumsy. When you have people sitting at a café table, a few squiggles will show their legs, no-one will count them.

Practice

There's really only one way to get confidence and fluidity into your figures – to sketch them constantly. A tiny sketchbook and a soft pencil used unobtrusively but often, in a café, in a car, at a bus station, anywhere, will produce wonders after a day or two. Your figures will begin to live, and you'll learn to produce them with fewer and fewer strokes of your pencil. Make them about 2.5–3.5cm (1-1½in) high, and with no more detail than I've shown below. Your confidence will increase rapidly, and you'll soon have a constant source of figures you can put into future paintings.

To show the importance of putting figures in your pictures, I've sketched a scene bereft of people. It looks too sterile. In the lower painting, I've added about 25 figures in different sizes. The figure size is a difficult problem with many painters, as a figure in one part of the painting looks too big and in another too small.

Of course the size of an adjacent door may be a help, but if you're still uncertain, try drawing your figure on tracing paper and moving it around your picture. You can tell when it fits comfortably. Scribble with a soft pencil on the other side of the tracing paper, and trace it on the painting with a ballpoint pen.

Notice how I've counterchanged the near figure's white shirt against the sea. Always try to put dark figures against a light background and vice versa.

Here are two deserted paintings for you to add figures. On the right is an empty square. I'd like you to add a couple of figures examining the wares in the foreground shop on the left. Like the shop itself, they would be almost silhouetted against the sunlit square. As for size, they should be able to go under the awning without banging their heads. Any figures on the opposite side of the square would have to be light against the dark, so you'll have to draw them first and paint the dark around them.

Another idea would be to create a crowd scene there – make it market day and fill it with shoppers with their carrier bags!

Copy this adding a figure coming round the distant corner. Here again the size is governed by the height of the door. Now add some ladies and children in their doorways, and finally a foreground figure by the side of the near wall. He or she would of course be larger, but the head although in proportion would be at the same level as the more distant figures – try including a dog too!

Flowers

One of my favourite flower painters, Charles Reed, once said that he actually knew very little about the flowers he paints so beautifully. He simply loved the patterns they make, as well as their wealth of texture and colour. Some of us may get caught up in too much botanical detail, which is fine in its place, but is not what we're aiming for here. We don't have to count petals and stamens to produce a fresh and satisfying picture. I see many flower paintings produced which are flat and boring, simply because the artist has forgotten all about counterchange, which is just as important in a bowl of flowers as it is in a landscape or street scene.

Design too is just as critical here as with any other subject. Dumping the nearest flowers in the nearest vessel and putting them in the middle of the paper simply won't do. After all, you've got much more control here over your subject matter than you have when you're painting a landscape. You can arrange the placing of light flowers against dark foliage, as well as your light source, before you start.

DO'S AND DONT'S

Do put light flowers against dark foliage.

Do put dark flowers against light background.

Do concentrate on making one flower dominant.

Do take time to arrange and light your flowers before you get your paints out. Informal balance is really important here.

Don't paint everything too flat.

Don't be afraid to experiment.

Opposite is a very informal and rapid painting of a few spring flowers in a jam jar, with the lighting coming from 2 o'clock. This shows an example of matching the flowers with the container. Here they fit in well. A dozen formal roses would need a much more elegant container. Remember, however, that the flowers are the stars of the picture. One side can be dark to throw up some light flowers, and the other side pale against some dark flowers.

This is my basic stroke for leaves. Hold the No 24 brush vertically to the paper. Using plenty of colour, press down on the paper with some pressure to create the wide part of the stroke, then take off the weight and flick the brush upwards in an arc to complete the stroke.

This is a basic flower stroke. Hold the brush at an angle of 45° to the paper. Try to put the flower in with a spontaneous sideways action. Once the paint is on the paper don't "worry" at it. Under these circumstances leave it looking fresh and transparent.

Hold the brush at a slight angle to the paper. Speed and lightness of touch are again paramount. This time it is the side of the brush which is used more. To produce the marks shown here a second, richer application of colour was laid over the first while it was still wet.

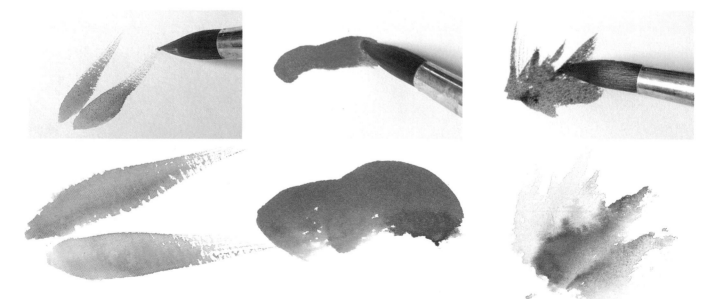

To try and enforce the discipline of simplicity on myself, I use a No 24 round brush, which has a superb point to allow a certain amount of delicacy without fiddling. Use the hake for backgrounds, and the No 3 rigger for stems, and very light foliage.

I still use my restricted seven colours. For instance, you can get beautiful mauves and purples by mixing alizarin crimson and ultramarine together. However, being completely sensible, I realize that in flower painting you sometimes need subtle, delicate shades, though I add colours such as cadmium orange, cadmium red and permanent rose, which in configuration with the rest should cover most flower needs.

Now back to setting up the arrangement. This is up to you own good taste and choice, but I find it works well if you have one or two large colourful and dramatic flowers, well counterchanged to form the point of interest, backed up by less demanding and delicate flowers and foliage. Once you are satisfied with the arrangement, the next task is to light it. The light at 10 o'clock or 2 o'clock usually works best.

Above is a simple set-up of fully blossomed roses in a pot. Paint the background first, picking out the white flowers by going round them, creating a negative shape. Then fill in the leaves with dark green to counterchange the flowers. The light is from top left.

Above is a very freely painted study using mainly lilacs and daffodils. The background is painted in very wet and the mauve, made from ultramarine and alizarin crimson, is dropped in immediately and allowed to diffuse. Then the yellow is painted straight from the tube. After this has dried, the dark foliage is painted in to sharpen and counterchange with the flowers.

These various single flowers and fruits can be copied to improve your skills with a large brush. Far better, however, would be to find similar things in your garden, and to try to paint them with as much economy of stroke as possible.

On these two pages I hope to get you to try yet another method of flower painting by producing abstract designs using wet into wet methods. With a little practice and experiment, you can really get exciting results, all you need is a little courage and imagination and lots of sheets of paper.

It's not difficult to design with flowers – in fact it's easier than any other subject. If your design needs a dark in a certain place – add a leaf! If you want a new light shape, wash it out with your hog's hair brush. A flower may be more beautiful than you can paint it, but with this method you can invent new ones by putting some neat, rich gorgeous colour on wet paper. You're never quite sure what is going to happen, which makes it so exciting. It's often a combination of how wet the paper is initially, how strongly the flowers are put into the wet, and how much calligraphy goes on when everything is dry.

Using a subtle wash, pick out the white rose shape and continue the wash to cover the bottom right area. While still wet, drop in strong cadmium red and alizarin and let it diffuse. When dry add foliage with sharp staccato strokes.

On the right, I have not attempted to show these flowers in any detail. It is an exercise in putting rich paint on to a large surface to get exciting effects. Once you get the idea, the possibilities are endless. Use neat paint on to the first damp wash.

The first stage is to apply a fairly weak wash. Try to avoid monotony by introducing various subtle colours.

Mix colour very thickly and while the first wash is still damp, paint in the basic rose shape using the second technique shown on p118, letting it diffuse into the first wash.

The third stage is to add rich, dark colour to indicate the petals before the second wash is dry. Finally, add the leaves using the first technique on p.118.

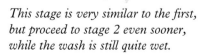

This stage is very similar to the first, but proceed to stage 2 even sooner, while the wash is still quite wet.

To compensate for the wetness of the first wash, the second application should be of almost neat paint. It will spread into the wet wash, but the strength of colour should remain.

While the second wash is still damp, mix up neat paynes grey and ultramarine, and drop it gently into the centre of the flower. This will diffuse, but only slightly.

Practice

Practice here using the large round brush and various techniques such as wet into wet. Also do some flower arranging yourself. This is very important in creating the finished painting. Keep counterchange constantly in mind, placing light-coloured flowers against dark foliage and darker flowers against a light background.

Copy these flowers, but use different colours. For example, try a white rose against a coloured background, then pick your own flowers and work directly.

Here I want you to set up your own flowers, using the painting on the right as a guide. Try arranging them differently but make sure they overlap slightly to keep them unified. Choose your own light direction.

124

Try painting the above bowl of flowers as it is, putting in the pink flowers first, and when dry, counterchange them with the green. You can then paint them again putting in a suitable background. Finally set up a similar group of flowers, and paint them directly using lighting from 10 o'clock.

Index

Acknowledgements

I would like to express my grateful thanks to Ann Mills, who has helped me enormously with the writing and Jenny Hickey who did all the typing from my almost indecipherable scribblings

LIST OF SUPPLIERS

Beaver Art & Framing Ltd,
Monk Street, Monmouth,
Gwent NP5 3NZ.
(Worldwide mail order service)

Berol Ltd,
Oldmedow Road,
King's Lynn,
Norfolk PE30 4JR
(Worldwide mail order service)

Daler-Rowney Ltd,
PO Box 10,
Bracknell,
Berkshire RG12 8ST.

Daler-Rowney Ltd (USA),
1085 Cranbury South River Road,
Demsburg,
New Jersey 08831,
USA.

Frisk Products Ltd,
7-1 Franthorne Way,
Randlesdown Road,
London SE6 3BT.

Frisk Products (USA) Inc.,
5240 Snapfinger Park Drive,
Suite 115,
Decatur,
Georgia 30035,
USA.

**Frisk Products
operate an export service:**
Clam Export Ltd,
48 Parsons Mead,
West Croydon,
CRO 3SL.

Pro Arte,
Sutton-in-Craven,
Nr. Keighley,
West Yorkshire BD20 7AX.

Pro Arte (USA),
PO Box 1043,
Big Timber,
Montana 59011,
USA.

Rexel Ltd,
Gatehouse Road,
Aylesbury,
Bucks HP19 3DT.
(and export)

Winsor & Newton,
Whitefriars Avenue,
Wealdstone,
Harrow,
Middlesex HA3 5RH.
(and export)